For Charlotte, Ben, Will and Eve

Praise for *Shelter*

'A mysterious old lady, a terrible evil, a courageous young hero, and a secret that could turn his world upside-down – the suspense never lets up. The ending will leave you breathless. I can't wait for Mickey Bolitar's next adventure.' Rick Riordan

'*Shelter* is a powerhouse thriller with a heart that beats like a triphammer. If you are looking for THE BOOK to get you hooked on reading, this is it. Pulses with excitement. *Shelter* will make your heart race long after the last page. Harlan Coben has created a hero worth following to hell and back.'

Eoin Colfer

Praise for Harlan Coben

'His trademark is twists that you don't see coming' *Daily Mail*

'A masterful balance of impeccable story-telling and flawless characterisation. There's no such thing as the perfect thriller, but Harlan Coben is as close as it gets.' *Daily Record*

'…Coben – possibly the most joyously readable crime writer in the world right now.' *Heat*

'If you haven't been caught by Coben's intelligent, gripping thrillers yet, this will hook you.' *Daily Mirror*

'*Caught* is a superb thriller… he has never written better.'

Evening Standard

'Coben's plots are always ingenious but that is never the point of them, so much as the emotional turmoil into which his characters are plunged.' *Independent*

'Bestselling writer Harlan Coben dazzles us yet again with a pacy thriller that's hard to put down.' *Star Magazine*

Also by Harlan Coben

HARLAN COBEN

shelter

A **MICKEY BOLITAR** NOVEL

First published in Great Britain in 2011 by Orion Books,
an imprint of The Orion Publishing Group Ltd
Orion House, 5 Upper Saint Martin's Lane
London WC2H 9EA

An Hachette UK Company

1 3 5 7 9 10 8 6 4 2

A CIP catalogue record for this book is
available from the British Library.

ISBN (Hardback): 978 1 4091 2445 0
ISBN (Export Trade Paperback): 978 1 4091 2446 7

Printed and bound by CPI Group (UK) Ltd, Croydon, CR0 4YY

The Orion Publishing Group's policy is to use papers that are natural,
renewable and recyclable products and made from wood grown in sustainable
forests. The logging and manufacturing processes are expected to
conform to the environmental regulations of the country of origin.

www.orionbooks.co.uk

shelter

chapter 1

I WAS WALKING TO SCHOOL, lost in feeling sorry for myself—my dad was dead, my mom in rehab, my girlfriend missing—when I saw the Bat Lady for the first time.

I had heard the rumors, of course. The Bat Lady supposedly lived alone in the dilapidated house on the corner of Hobart Gap Road and Pine. You know the one. I stood in front of it now. The worn yellow paint was shedding like an old dog. The once-solid concrete walk was cracked into quarter-size fragments. The uncut lawn had dandelions tall enough for the adult rides at Six Flags.

The Bat Lady was said to be a hundred years old and only came out at night, and if some poor child hadn't made it home from a playdate or practice at the Little League field before nightfall—if he or she risked walking home in the dark instead of getting a ride, or was maybe crazy enough to cut through her yard—the Bat Lady got you.

What she supposedly did with you was never made clear. No child had vanished from this town in years. Teenagers, like my girlfriend, Ashley, sure, they could be here one day, holding your hand, looking deep into your eyes, making your heart go *boom-boom-boom*—and be gone the next. But little kids? Nope. They were safe, even from the Bat Lady.

So I was just about to cross to the other side of the street—even I, a mature teenager entering my sophomore year at a brand-new high school, wanted to avoid that spooky house—when the door creaked open.

I froze.

For a moment, nothing happened. The door was all the way open now, but no one was there. I stopped and waited. Maybe I blinked. I can't be sure.

But when I looked again, the Bat Lady was there.

She could have been a hundred years old. Or maybe two hundred. I had no idea why they called her Bat Lady. She didn't look like a bat. Her hair was gray and hippie long, hanging down to her waist. It blew in the wind, obscuring her face. She wore a torn white gown that resembled a bridal costume in an old horror movie or heavy-metal video. Her spine was bent like a question mark.

Slowly Bat Lady raised a hand so pale it was more vein-blue than white, and pointed a shaky, bony finger in my direction. I said nothing. She kept pointing until she was sure

I was looking. When she saw that I was, Bat Lady's wrinkled face spread into a smile that sent little icicles down my spine.

"Mickey?"

I had no idea how she knew my name.

"Your father isn't dead," Bat Lady said.

Her words sent a jolt that knocked me back a step.

"He is very much alive."

But standing there, watching her vanish back into her decrepit cave, I knew what she was telling me wasn't true.

Because I had seen my father die.

Okay, that was weird.

I stood in front of Bat Lady's house and waited for her to come back out. No go. I walked over to her door and looked for a doorbell. There was none, so I started pounding on the door. It shook under the onslaught. The wood was so rough it scraped my knuckles like sandpaper. Paint chips fell off as if the door had a bad case of dandruff.

But the Bat Lady did not appear.

So now what? Kick down the door . . . and then what? Find an old lady in a weird white dress and demand she explain her whack-a-doodle rants? Maybe she had gone upstairs. Maybe Bat Lady was now getting ready for her loony day, changing out of her white dress, heading to the shower . . .

Ugh.

Time to go. I didn't want to miss the first bell anyway. My homeroom teacher, Mr. Hill, was a stickler for punctuality.

Plus I still hoped that Ashley would show up today. She had vanished into thin air. Maybe she would just reappear the same way.

I met Ashley three weeks ago at high school orientation for both new kids (Ashley and me, for example) and incoming freshmen, all of whom already knew one another because they went to middle school and elementary school together. No one ever seems to leave this town.

An orientation should consist of visiting your classes, getting a tour of the facilities, and maybe meeting a few classmates. But no, that's not enough. We had to participate in these moronic, dehumanizing, and totally awkward "team building" exercises.

The first involved the "trust fall." Ms. Owens, a PE teacher with a smile that looked like it'd been painted on by a drunk clown, started off by trying to fire us up.

"Good morning, everyone!"

A few groans.

Then—and I hate when adults do this—she shouted, "I know you're more excited than that, so let's try it again! Good morning, everyone!"

The students yelled "Good morning" louder this time, not because they were excited but because they wanted her to stop.

We were broken down into groups of six—mine featured three incoming freshmen and three upperclassmen who had just moved to town.

"One of you will stand on this pedestal and wear a blindfold!" Ms. Owens exclaimed. Everything she said ended in an exclamation mark. "You will cross your arms and now I want you to pretend that the pedestal is on fire! Oh no!" Ms. Owens put her hands on her cheeks like the kid in *Home Alone*. "It's so hot that you'll have to fall back!"

Someone raised his hand. "Why would we keep our arms crossed if the pedestal was on fire?"

Murmurs of agreement.

Ms. Owens's painted-on smile didn't change, but I thought I noticed a twitch in her right eye. "Your arms are tied!"

"They are? No, they're not."

"Pretend!"

"But if we pretend that, why do we need the blindfold? Can't we just pretend not to see?"

"Or close our eyes?"

Ms. Owens fought for control. "The pedestal is so hot from the fire that you fall backward off of it."

"Backward?"

"Wouldn't we jump, Ms. Owens?"

"Really. Why would we fall backward? I mean, if it's that hot."

Ms. Owens had enough. "Because I say so! You will fall backward! The rest of the group will catch you! Then you'll switch places until everyone has a turn falling backward!"

We all did this, though some of us were hesitant. I'm six-four and weigh two hundred pounds. The group winced when they saw me. Another girl in my group, an incoming freshman dressed all in black, was on the fat side. I know I should call her something other than fat, something more politically correct, but I'm not sure what without sounding condescending. Large? Chubby? Heavy? I say those without judgment, the same way I might say small, bony, or skinny.

The big girl hesitated before she climbed onto the pedestal. Someone in our group laughed. Then someone else.

Other than to show this girl that cruelty will not stop when you enter high school, I had no idea how this exercise was supposed to help anyone.

When the girl didn't fall back right away, one of the freshman boys snickered and said, "C'mon, Ema. We'll catch you."

It was not a voice that gave her confidence. She pulled down her blindfold and looked back at us. I met her eye and nodded. Finally she let herself fall. We caught her—some adding dramatic grunts—but Ema didn't look any more trusting.

We then played some dumb paintball game where two people got hurt and then we moved into an exercise called— I wish I were kidding—"Poisoned Peanut Butter." For this event, you had to cross over a ten-yard patch of Poisoned Peanut Butter but, as Ms. Owens explained, "Only two of you can wear the Anti-Poison shoes to get across at a time!"

In short, you had to carry other team members on your back. The small girls laughed with a tee-hee as they were carried. A photographer with the *Star-Ledger* newspaper was there, snapping away. The reporter asked a glowing Ms. Owens questions, her answers filled with words like *bonding, welcoming, trusting*. I couldn't imagine what sort of story you'd do on something like this, but maybe they were desperate for "human interest" material.

I stood in the back of the Poisoned Peanut Butter line with Ema. Black mascara was running down her face with what might have been silent tears. I wondered if the photographer would get that.

As it came closer to Ema's turn for teammates to carry her across the Poisoned Peanut Butter, I could actually feel her start to shake in fear.

Think about it.

It's your first day at a new school and you're a girl who weighs probably two hundred pounds and you're forced to put on gym shorts and then, to complete some inane group task, your new smaller classmates have to lug you like a beer keg for ten yards while you just want to curl up in a ball and die.

Who thinks this is a good idea?

Ms. Owens came over to our team. "Ready, Emma?!"

Ema (with a long *e*) or Emma. I didn't know what her name was now.

Emma/Ema said nothing.

"You go, girl! Right across the Poisoned Peanut Butter! You can do it!"

Then I said, "Ms. Owens?"

She turned her gaze on me. The smile never changed, but the eyes narrowed slightly. "And you are?"

"My name is Mickey Bolitar. I'm an incoming sophomore. And I'm going to sit out this exercise, if it's okay."

Again the flutter in Ms. Owens's right eye. "Excuse me?"

"Yeah, I don't really think I'm up for being carried."

The other kids looked at me like I had a third arm growing out of my forehead.

"Mr. Bolitar, you're new here." The exclamation point was gone from Ms. Owens's voice. "I would think you'd want to participate."

"Is it mandatory?" I asked.

"Excuse me?"

"Is participating in this particular exercise mandatory?"

"Well, no, it's not manda—"

"Then I'm sitting out." I looked over at Ema/Emma. "Would you mind keeping me company?"

We walked away then. Behind me I could hear the world go silent. Then Ms. Owens blew a whistle, stopping the exercise and calling for lunch.

When we were a few more feet away, Ema/Emma said, "Wow."

"What?"

She looked me straight in the eye. "You saved the fat girl. I bet you're really proud of yourself."

Then she shook her head and walked away.

I looked behind me. Ms. Owens watched us. She still had the smile, but the glare in her eyes made it clear that I'd managed to make an enemy my first day.

The sun beat down upon me. I let it. I closed my eyes for a moment. I thought about my mother, who was coming home from rehab soon. I thought about my father, who was dead and buried.

I felt very much alone.

The school cafeteria was closed—school opening was still weeks away—so we all had to bring our own. I bought a buffalo chicken sub at Wilkes Deli and sat by myself on a grassy hill overlooking the football field. I was about to bite into it when I noticed her.

She wasn't my type, though I really don't have a type. I've spent my entire life traveling overseas. My parents worked for a charitable foundation in places like Laos and Peru and Sierra Leone. I don't have any siblings. It was exciting and fun when I was a kid, but it got tiresome and difficult as I grew older. I wanted to stay in one place. I wanted to make some friends and play on one basketball team and, well, meet girls and do teenage stuff. It's hard to do that when you're backpacking in Nepal.

This girl was very pretty, sure, but she was also prim and proper and preppy. Something about her looked stuck-up, though I couldn't say what. Her hair was the pale blond of a porcelain doll. She wore an actual, well, skirt, not one of those short-short ones, and what might have been bobby socks, and looked as though she'd just walked out of my grandparents' Brooks Brothers catalog.

I took a bite of my sandwich and then I noticed that she didn't have a lunch. Maybe she was on some kind of weird diet, but for some reason I didn't think so.

I don't know why, but I decided to walk over to her. I wasn't much in the mood to talk or to meet anyone. I was still reeling from all the new people in my life and really didn't want to add any more.

Maybe it was just because she was so pretty. Maybe I'm just as shallow as the next guy. Or maybe it was because the lonely can sometimes sense the lonely. Maybe what drew me to her was the fact that, like me, she seemed to want to keep to herself.

I approached tentatively. When I got close enough, I gave a half wave and said, "Hi."

I always open with super-smooth lines like this.

She looked up at me and shaded eyes the green of emeralds. "Hi."

Yep, very pretty.

I stood there, feeling awkward. My face reddened. My hands suddenly felt too big for my body. The second thing I said to her was, "My name is Mickey."

Man, am I smooth or what? Every line is killer.

"I'm Ashley Kent."

"Cool," I said.

"Yeah."

Somewhere in this world—in China or India or a remote section of Africa—there was probably a bigger dork than me. But I couldn't swear to that.

I pointed at her empty lap. "Did you bring lunch?"

"No, I forgot."

"This sandwich is huge," I said. "Do you want half?"

"Oh, I couldn't."

But I insisted and then she invited me to join her. Ashley was also a sophomore and also new in town. Her father, she said, was a renowned surgeon. Her mother was a lawyer.

If life were a movie, this was the part where you'd start the music montage. Some sappy song would be playing while they flashed to Ashley and me sharing lunch, talking, laughing, looking coy, holding hands—and ending with that first chaste kiss.

That was three weeks ago.

I made it into Mr. Hill's class just as the bell sounded. He took roll call. The bell pealed again, and it was time for first period. Ashley's homeroom was across the hall. I waited and saw that yet again she wasn't here.

I described Ashley before as my girlfriend. That might have been an exaggeration. We were taking it slow, I guess. We'd kissed twice—no more. I didn't really like anyone else at my new school. I liked her. It wasn't love. But it was also early. On the other hand, feelings like this usually diminish. That's the truth. We like to pretend that they grow as we get closer to our new partner. But most times, it's the opposite. We guys see that gorgeous girl and we get this big-time crush, one that makes it hard to breathe and makes us so anxious, want it so bad, that we always blow it.

If we do somehow land her, the feelings begin to diminish almost immediately. In this case, my feelings for Ashley really did grow. That was a little scary in a good way.

Then one day I came to school and Ashley was absent. I tried her cell phone, but there was no answer. She was gone the next day too. Then the next. I wasn't sure what to do. I didn't have her home address. I checked the name Kent online, but they must have been unlisted. In fact, there was nothing about her online at all.

Ashley had simply vanished into thin air.

chapter 2

AN IDEA CAME TO ME during third period.

Ashley and I had only one class together—AP History with Mrs. Friedman. She was my favorite teacher so far. She was theatrical and enthusiastic. Today she was talking about how well-rounded certain historical figures were, begging us to become "Renaissance men or women."

I hadn't talked to her privately yet. I hadn't talked to any of my teachers outside of class. I'd kept to myself. That was my way. I know I got "new kid" stares. One day, a group of girls were giggling in my direction. One came up to me and said, "Can I, like, have your phone number?"

Confused, I gave it to her.

Five minutes later I heard giggling and my phone vibrated. The text read: **My friend thinks you're cute.** I didn't respond.

After class, I approached Mrs. Friedman.

"Ah, Mr. Bolitar," Mrs. Friedman said with a smile that lit up her face. "I'm glad to have you in my class."

I wasn't sure how to reply to that, so I went with, "Uh, thank you."

"I never had your father," she said, "but your uncle was one of my favorite students. You resemble him."

My uncle. The great Myron Bolitar. I didn't like my uncle and was really tired of hearing how swell he was. My father and my uncle were very close growing up, but then they had a major falling-out. For the last fifteen years of my dad's life—basically from the moment I was conceived to the moment he died—the two brothers hadn't spoken. I guess I should forgive Uncle Myron, but I'm not much in the mood.

"What can I do for you, Mr. Bolitar?"

When some teachers call you Mister or Miz, it comes across as either patronizing or too formal. Mrs. Friedman hit the right note.

"As you probably know," I said slowly, "Ashley Kent has been absent."

"And so she has." Mrs. Friedman was a short woman and it took some effort for her to look all the way up at me. "You two are close."

"We're friends."

"Oh, come, Mr. Bolitar. I may be old, but I see the way you look at her. Even Ms. Caldwell is upset she isn't catching your eye."

I reddened when she said this. Rachel Caldwell was probably the hottest girl in the school.

"Anyway," I said, dragging out the word, "I was thinking
maybe I could help her out."

"Help her out how?"

"I thought maybe I could get her homework and then,
you know, pass it on to her."

Mrs. Friedman had been cleaning off the blackboard. Most
teachers used a Smart Board, but as Mrs. Friedman liked to
joke, she was "old-school—literally." She stopped and looked
at me. "Did Ashley ask you to get her homework?"

"Well, no."

"So you just took it upon yourself?"

This was a dumb idea. Even if she did give me the homework, where would I bring it? I didn't know where Ashley
lived. "Never mind," I said. "Thanks anyway."

She put down the eraser. "Mr. Bolitar?"

I turned back to her.

"Do you know why Ashley Kent has been absent?"

My heart started doing a slow thud. "No, ma'am."

"But you're worried."

I didn't see any point in lying to her. "Yes, ma'am."

"She hasn't called you?"

"No, she hasn't."

"Strange." Mrs. Friedman frowned. "All I can tell you is
that I got a note saying that I shouldn't expect Ashley back."

"I'm not sure I understand."

15

"That's all I know," Mrs. Friedman said. "I guess she moved away. But . . ."

Her voice trailed off.

"But what?"

"Never mind, Mr. Bolitar." She started wiping the blackboard again. "Just . . . just be careful."

At lunchtime I waited on line at the cafeteria.

I always figured that there would be more drama to a high school cafeteria. Yes, it was full of cliques. The jocks here were called "Lax Bros" (Lacrosse Brothers). They all had long hair, big muscles, and started every sentence with the word *Yah*. There was a table for the "Animes"—white kids who think they're Asian. They loved manga comics and video games that matched. The pretty girls weren't so much pretty as skinny with too-high heels and expensive clothes. Then there were the gamers, the hipsters, the skaters, the druggies, the geeks, the theater kids.

There didn't seem to be much class warfare here. These kids had been together for so long that they didn't really notice. The so-called outcasts who sat alone had been sitting alone for so many years that it wasn't so much cruelty as habit. I wasn't sure if that was better or worse.

A kid who would definitely fit into the geek camp came up to me with a tray in his hand. His pant cuffs were set at flood level. His sneakers were pure white with no logo.

He pushed up his Harry Potter glasses and lifted his tray in my direction.

"Hey, you want my spoon?" he asked me. "I barely used it."

I looked at the tray. "Barely?"

"Yeah."

He raised the tray a little higher so I could see. The spoon sat in his syrupy fruit cup.

"No," I said, "I'm good."

"You sure?"

"Are they out of spoons or something?"

"Nah. They got plenty."

Oookay. "Then thanks, no, I'm good."

He shrugged. "Suit yourself."

When I finished buying lunch, Spoon—that was how I thought of him now—was waiting for me.

"Where you going to sit?" he asked.

Since Ashley had vanished, I'd been eating alone outside. "I'm not sure."

Spoon started to follow me. "You're big and you keep to yourself. Like Shrek."

Not much to say to that.

"I could be your Donkey. You know?"

Oookay. If I went outside, he'd follow, so I looked for a safe place inside to sit.

"Or your Robin. Like Batman and Robin. Or Sancho

17

Panza. You ever read *Don Quixote*? Me neither, but I saw the musical *Man of La Mancha*. I love musicals. So does my dad. My mom, not so much. She likes cage fighting, like the MMA. That's Mixed Martial Arts. Dad and me, we go to a musical once a month. Do you like musicals?"

"Sure," I said, scanning the cafeteria for a safe haven.

"My dad's cool like that. Taking me to musicals and stuff. We've seen *Mamma Mia* three times. It's awesome. The movie, not so much. I mean, Pierce Brosnan sings like someone shot him in the throat with an arrow. Dad gets discount tickets because he works at the school. He's the janitor here. But don't ask him to give you access to the girls' locker room, okay? Because I asked and he said no dice. Dad can be strict like that, you know?"

"Yeah," I said. "I know."

There was a nearly empty table in the so-called outcast corner. The only person sitting there was my unappreciative damsel in distress—Ema or Emma—I still hadn't learned her name.

"So about being your Donkey?"

"I'll get back to you," I told Spoon.

I hurried over and put my tray next to hers. She had the heavy black makeup thing going on, shoe-polish black hair, black clothes, black boots, pale skin. She was goth or emo or whatever they called that look now. Tattoos covered her forearms. One snaked up her shirt and around her neck. She looked up at me with a face that could not look more sullen without actually being punched.

"Oh, great," she said. "The pity sit."

"Pity sit?"

"Think about it."

I did. I had never heard that one before. "Oh, I get it. Like I pity you for sitting alone. So I sit with you."

She rolled her eyes. "And here I pegged you for a dumb jock."

"I'm trying to be a Renaissance man."

"You have Mrs. Friedman too, I see." She looked to her left, then her right. "Where's your preppy girlfriend?"

"I don't know."

"So from sitting with the prissy pretty girl to sitting with me." Ema/Emma shook her head. "Talk about a big step down." L207,066

I was getting tired of thinking of her as Ema/Emma. "What's your name?"

"Why do you want to know?"

"I heard a kid call you Ema. I heard Ms. Owens call you Emma."

She picked up her fork and started playing with her food. I noticed now that she had pierced eyebrows. Ouch. "My real first name is Emma. But everyone calls me Ema."

"Why? I just want to know what to call you."

Grudgingly, she said, "Ema."

"Okay. Ema."

She played with her food some more. "So what's your deal? I mean, when you're not rescuing the fat girl."

"Your bitter act," I said. "It's a little over the top."

"You think?"

"I would dial it back."

She shrugged. "You might be right. So you're a new kid, right?"

"I am."

"Where you from?"

"We traveled around at lot," I said. "How about you?"

She grimaced. "I've lived in this town my whole life."

"Doesn't seem to be too bad."

"I don't see you fitting in yet."

"I don't want to fit in."

Ema liked that reply. I looked down at my tray. I picked up my spoon and thought of, well, Spoon. I shook my head and smiled.

"What?" Ema asked.

"Nothing."

It was weird to think about this, but when my father was my age, he sat in this very cafeteria and ate his lunch. He was young and had his whole life ahead of him. I glanced around the room and wondered where he would have sat, who he would've talked to, if he laughed as easily back then as when I'd known him.

These thoughts became like a giant hand pushing down on my chest. I blinked and put down the spoon.

"Hey, you okay?" Ema asked.

"Fine."

I thought about Bat Lady and what she had said to me. Crazy ol' bat—hey, maybe that's where she got the nickname. You don't just get a rep like hers for nothing. You get it for doing crazy things. Like telling a boy who saw his father die in a car crash that the man he missed so much was still alive.

I flashed to the day just eight months ago when we landed in Los Angeles—my father, my mother, and me. My parents wanted to give me a place where I could go to high school and play for a real basketball team and maybe go to college.

Nice plans, right?

Now my dad was dead and my mother was shattered.

"Ema?" I said.

She looked at me warily.

"Do you know anything about the Bat Lady?"

Ema frowned. When she did, the mascara on her eyes folded up and then spread out like a fan. "Now I get it."

"What?"

"Why you sat here," Ema said. "You figured—what?— the crazy fat girl would know all about the crazy old Bat Lady."

"What? No."

Ema rose with her tray. "Just leave me alone, okay?"

"No, wait, you don't understand—"

"I understand fine. You did your good deed."

"Will you stop that? Ema?"

She hurried away. I took a step to follow her and stopped. Two big muscle-heads wearing varsity football jackets snickered. One came up on my right, the other on my left. The one on my right—the name stenciled in cursive on his chest was BUCK—slapped me too hard on the shoulder and said, "Looks like you struck out, huh?"

The other muscle-head—stenciled name: TROY—laughed at that. "Yeah," Troy said. "Struck out. With the fat chick."

Back to Buck: "Fat and ugly."

Troy: "And you still struck out."

"Dude."

Buck and Troy high-fived each other. Then they turned and put their hands up for me to high-five. Buck said, "Up top, bro."

I frowned. "Don't you guys have a steroid needle that needs an ass cheek?"

Their mouths both formed surprise Os. I pushed past them. Buck called out, "We ain't done with this, dead man."

"Yeah," Troy added, "dead man."

"Totally dead."

"Dead man."

Man, I hoped that nickname didn't stick.

As I chased after Ema, I saw Ms. Owens, who was working as cafeteria monitor, move quickly to cut me off. There was a gleam in her eyes. Ms. Owens hadn't forgiven me for the team-building fiasco. Still with the painted smile, she got right up in my face and blew her whistle.

"We don't run in the cafeteria," she said, "or we get a week's detention. Do I make myself clear?"

I looked around me. Buck made a gun with his finger and dropped the hammer. Ema dumped her tray and headed through the doors. Ms. Owens smiled and dared me to run after her. I didn't.

Yep, I was making friends fast.

chapter 3

MY COMBINATION LOCK NEVER OPENS on the first try. I don't know why.

I had just done the numbers: 14, back to 7, over to 28 . . . Nope, it didn't open. I was about to try again when I heard a now-familiar voice say, "I collect bobble-heads."

I turned to see Spoon.

"Good to know," I said.

Spoon gestured for me to move out of the way. He pulled out a huge key ring, found the one he was looking for, and stuck it in the back of my lock. The lock opened, presto.

"What's your combination?" he asked me.

I said, "Umm, should I tell you?"

"Hello?" Spoon jangled his keys in my face. "You think I need your combination to break in?"

"Good point." I told him the numbers. He fiddled with the lock and handed it back to me. "It should work with no problems now."

He started to leave.

"Wait, Spoon?"

He turned toward me. "What did you call me?"

"Sorry, I don't know your name."

"Spoon," he said, looking up and smiling as though trying the word out for the first time. "I like it. Spoon. Yeah. Call me Spoon, okay?"

"Sure"—he looked at me so expectantly—"uh, Spoon." He beamed. I wasn't sure how to ask this, but I figured what the heck. "You have a lot of keys there."

"Don't call me Keys, okay? I prefer Spoon."

"Yeah, of course. Spoon it is. You said before that your dad is the janitor here, right?"

"Right. By the way, the White Witch in the Narnia series? I think she's sexy as all get out."

"Yeah, me too," I said, trying to get him back on track. "Can your dad really get you into locked places in the school?"

Spoon smiled. "Sure, but I don't really need to ask my dad. I got the keys here." He dangled them in case I didn't know what keys he meant. "But we can't go in the girls' locker room. I asked him about that—"

"Right, no, not the girls' locker room. But you can get into other places?"

Spoon pushed the glasses back up his nose. "Why? What do you have in mind?"

"Well," I said, "I was wondering if we could get into the main office and check a student's file."

"What student?" he asked.

"Her name is Ashley Kent."

School ends at three P.M., but Spoon told me that the coast wouldn't be clear until seven. That gave me four hours to kill. It was too early to visit Mom—I was only allowed night visits because Mom was supposedly working on her rehabilitation during the day—so I headed back to Bat Lady's house.

As I walked out of the school, I noticed a voice mail. My guess was it was from an adult. Kids text. Adults leave voice mails, which are a pain because you have to call in and go through the prompts and then listen to the messages and then delete them.

Yep, I was right. The message was from my uncle Myron. "I booked our flight to Los Angeles for first thing Saturday morning," he said in his most somber voice. "We'll fly in, then back the next day."

Los Angeles. We were flying out to see my father's grave. Myron had never seen the final resting place of his brother. My grandparents, who would meet us out there, had never seen the resting place of their youngest son.

Uncle Myron went on: "I got a ticket for your mother, of

course. She can't be left on her own. I know you two want a private reunion tomorrow, but maybe I should be around, you know, just in case."

I frowned. No way.

"Anyway, hope you're fine. I'm around tonight if you want to grab a pizza or something."

I didn't feel like calling, so I sent a quick text: **Won't be home for dinner. I think it will be less stressful on Mom if you're not around.**

Myron wouldn't like it, but too bad. He wasn't my legal guardian. That was part of the deal we struck. When he found out that my father was dead and that my mom was having problems, he threatened to sue for custody. I countered that if he did that, I'd run away—I still have enough connections overseas—or I would sue for emancipation.

My mom may have some issues, but she's still my mom.

It wasn't a pretty fight, but in the end, we came up with, if not an agreement, a cease-fire. I agreed to live in his house in Kasselton, New Jersey. It was the same house both Myron and my dad grew up in. Yes, that was weird. I use the basement bedroom, which had been Myron's room, and do all I can to avoid the upstairs room where my father spent his childhood. Still it's a little creepy.

Anyway, in return for agreeing to live in the house, Myron agreed to let my mother remain my sole guardian and, well, to leave me alone. That was the part he had trouble handling.

When I looked now at Bat Lady's house, I shivered. The

wind had picked up, bending the bare trees in her yard. I had seen every kind of superstition in all four corners of the globe. Most seemed downright silly, though my parents always told me to keep an open mind. I didn't believe in haunted houses. I didn't believe in ghosts or spirits or things that go bump in the night.

But if I did, man, this place had them all.

The place was so dilapidated it actually seemed to lean, like if you pushed too hard it might just crumble to the ground. There were loose boards. Some windows were gone, replaced with wooden planks. The ones that remained were fogged up as if the house just took a hot shower, which, judging by the dirt, wasn't really possible.

If I hadn't seen her with my own eyes, I would swear the house had been abandoned for years.

I approached again and knocked on the door. No answer. I put my ear close to the panel—not too close because I didn't want to get a splinter—and listened. Nothing. Not a sound. I knocked some more. Still no answer.

So now what?

What could I really do here? Something. Anything. I decided to try the back door. I circled to the left because, like I said, the house tilted and if it suddenly collapsed, I didn't want it to fall on me. I looked up. There was a widow's peak way up high and for a moment I imagined the Bat Lady sitting up there in a rocking chair, still dressed in white, looking down at me.

I hurried my steps, wondering what I'd find in her back-yard.

Nothing.

The house came right up against the woods. It was the strangest thing. It was as though the house was built half onto a plot of land, half in a forest, like it was emerging from the trees. From the street, it just looked as if maybe there were a ton of trees in her backyard. But it was all trees. The roots seemed to merge right into the foundation. Thick, ugly vines ran up the back walls. I don't know if the house was originally built in the woods and then a clearing was made in the front, or if it was the opposite, if the woods behind it had sneaked up and started to swallow Bat Lady's house whole.

"What are you doing?"

I bit back a scream and jumped high enough to dunk a basketball. The voice had come from behind me. I spun quickly, taking two steps back and banging into a tree.

It was Ema.

"Scared you, huh?" She laughed and lifted her arms into wings. "Did you think I was the Bat Lady coming to take you away?"

My voice was a whisper. "Knock it off."

"Big tough guy."

"What are you doing here anyway?" I asked.

She shrugged.

"Wait, were you following me?"

"Really, Mickey?" She put her hands on her hips. "Conceited much?"

I wasn't sure what to say to that.

"It was just . . ." Ema sighed. "You mentioned Bat Lady. And you came to my rescue, right, and then I guess I just got curious."

"So you followed me here?"

Ema didn't reply. She looked around as though she'd just realized that we were half in the woods, half leaning against the back of Bat Lady's house. "So why are you here anyway? No luck with the fat chick, so you figured you'd try the old one?"

I just looked at her.

"I heard what they said. Buck and Troy. They've been on me for so long it's hard to remember a time when they weren't." She turned away, bit her lower lip, and then faced me again. "I also heard they threatened you for defending me."

I shrugged it off.

"So what are you doing here?"

I wondered how to explain it and went with the simple: "I want to talk to Bat Lady."

Ema smiled. "No, seriously."

"I am serious."

"No, you're not. Because, well, she's not real. Bat Lady's just a myth the big kids use to scare the little kids. I mean, I don't know anyone who has ever seen her."

30

"I've seen her," I said.

"When?"

"This morning." Then I added: "She told me that my father was still alive."

Ema looked puzzled.

"He died in a car crash earlier this year," I explained.

"Whoa," Ema said, her eyes going wide. "I'm not sure what to say to that."

"I just want to talk to her."

"Okay, I get it. I saw you knock on her door. So what's your plan now?"

"Try the back door."

"Makes sense, I guess," Ema said. She looked toward the woods and narrowed her eyes. "Look at that."

She pointed into the woods and took a few steps in that direction. I didn't see anything other than trees.

"There's a road back there," Ema said. "Maybe a building." I still didn't see it. She walked toward it. I followed her. A few steps later, I could see that she was right. There, maybe fifty yards behind Bat Lady's house, was what might have been a garage, painted in a brown-green that worked as camouflage. There was a dirt road from somewhere in the woods leading up to it. You couldn't see either one from the front of the house. Heck, you couldn't even see them from the back door.

Ema bent down and touched the dirt. "Tire tracks for a car," she said, like she was following someone in an old movie. "This must be how Bat Lady goes in and out—through this dirt road. She can park and go in and no one would ever see her."

"Bat Lady drives?"

"What, you think she flies?"

I felt a chill. The garage was in better shape than the house but not by much. I tried the garage door. It too was locked. There were no windows, so I couldn't see if there was a car inside.

I didn't know what to make of all this. Probably nothing. An eccentric old woman lived here. She liked to go in and out through a private entrance. Big deal. There was no reason for me to be here.

Except, of course, she had known my name. And there was that bit about my father being alive . . .

Who says that to someone? Your father's still alive? Who does that?

Enough. I spun around and headed to the back door. I knocked. No reply. I knocked harder. There were dirty windows on the door. I cupped my hands around my eyes to look inside, and while I did, I felt the door give way just a little. I looked down at the knob. Decay had eaten away at the doorjamb. I reached into my pocket and pulled out my wallet. Ema was by my side now. I extracted a credit card, hiding the name on it from her.

"Whoa," she said. "You know how to break in?"

"No, but I've seen it on TV. You just sort of slide the card."

She frowned. "And you think that'll work?"

"Normally no," I said. "But look how old that lock is. It looks like it'll break if I breathe on it too hard."

"Okay, but think it through first."

"Huh?"

"Suppose the door does open," Ema said. "Then what?"

I wasn't thinking that far ahead. I jammed the credit card into the opening in the jamb. I slid it down. It met resistance. I slid a little harder. Nothing. I was about to give up when the door slowly opened with a creak noisy enough to echo into the woods.

"Whoa," Ema said again.

I pushed the door the rest of the way open. The creak grew louder, causing birds to scatter. Ema put her hand on my forearm. I looked down and saw her fingernails were black. She had silver rings on every finger. One was a skull and crossbones.

"That's breaking and entering," she said.

"You going to call the cops?" I asked.

"You kidding?" Her eyes lit up. She looked younger now, sweeter, almost like a little kid. When I saw the hint of a smile, I arched an eyebrow and that, I guessed, scared it away. The sullen was back. "Whatever," she said, trying to sound like she couldn't care less. "It's cool."

No, not cool. I knew that this wasn't the smartest move, but the need to do something here, anything, outweighed those personal concerns. Besides, really, what was the risk?

33

An old woman had yelled out some crazy things to me in the morning. I came by to check on her. When there was no answer, I decided to make sure that she was okay. That would be my story. What were they going to do, lock me up for that?

"You might as well go home," I said to her.

"Dream on."

"I guess I could use a lookout."

"I'd rather go in."

I shook my head.

Ema sighed. "Fine. I'll be the lookout." She took out her cell phone. "What's your number?"

I gave it to her.

"I'll stand over there. If I see her flap her wings, I'll text you. By the way, what are you going to do if she is inside, waiting in the dark to pounce on you?"

I didn't bother replying, though in truth I hadn't thought of that. What if Bat Lady was waiting for me and . . . and what? What was she going to do, jump on my back? I'm a six-foot-four-inch teenager. She's a tiny old woman. Get a grip.

I stepped into the kitchen. I didn't close the door behind me. I wanted a quick escape in case . . . well, whatever.

The kitchen was from another era. I remember once watching a rerun of a black-and-white TV show called *The Honeymooners* with my dad. I didn't really think it was very funny. A lot of the humor seemed to come from Ralph threatening to physically abuse his wife, Alice. Ralph and

Alice had a refrigerator—if that's what this was—like this one. Bat Lady's linoleum floor was the dirty yellow of a smoker's teeth. A cuckoo clock was stopped on the wrong time, the bird out of his little brown house. The cuckoo looked cold.

"Hello?" I called out. "Anyone home?"

Not a sound.

I should just leave. Really. What was I looking for?

Your father isn't dead. He is very much alive.

On the one hand, I knew better. I had been in that car with my father. I saw him die. On the other hand . . . you just don't say a thing like that and not expect a son to demand an explanation.

I tiptoed across the peeling tiles. I passed a checkerboard tablecloth like something you'd see at a pizza joint. There were salt and pepper shakers stuck to it, the contents hardened. I stepped out of the kitchen and stopped in front of a spiral staircase leading up to the second floor.

Where, no doubt, Bat Lady's bedroom was.

"Hello?"

No reply.

I put one foot on the first step. Then those images—the ones of Bat Lady maybe getting dressed or showering—filled my head. I put my foot back down on the first floor. Uh-uh. I wasn't going up. At least, not right now.

I entered the living room. It was dark. The key color: brown. Very little illumination made it through the dirt and wood covering the windows. There was a tall grandfather clock, also not working. I spotted an old-fashioned cabinet stereo. A hi-fi, I think they called it. It had a turntable on top. Vinyl albums were stacked to the side. I spotted *Pet Sounds* by the Beach Boys, the Beatles walking across Abbey Road, and *My Generation* by the Who.

I tried picturing Bat Lady blasting classic rock in this dark room. The image was simply too weird.

I stopped and listened again. Nothing. Across the room I spotted a giant fireplace. The mantel was bare except for one photograph. I began to move toward it when something made me pull up.

There was a record on the turntable.

I took another look. I knew this particular record well. This record—the one Bat Lady had most recently played— was called *Aspect of Juno* by a group called HorsePower. My parents listened to it a lot. Years ago, when Mom and Dad first met, my mother was friends with Gabriel Wire and Lex Ryder, the two guys who made up HorsePower. Sometimes, when Dad was traveling, I would find Mom listening to the music alone and crying.

I swallowed. A coincidence?

Of course it was. HorsePower was still a popular group. Lots of people owned their music. So it happened to be sitting on Bat Lady's turntable—big deal, right?

Except it *was* a big deal. I just didn't see how yet.

Keep moving, I thought.

I started again toward the photograph on the mantel. The fireplace itself was filled with soot and burnt, yellowed newspaper. I lifted the picture gently from the mantel, afraid that it might fall apart with a mere touch of my hands. It didn't. The glass on the frame was so thick with dust that I tried to blow it clean. Dumb move. The dust flew into my eyes and up my nose. I sneezed. My eyes watered. When they stopped, I blinked my eyes open and looked down at the photograph in my hand.

Hippies.

There were five of them in the picture: three women, two men, and they were standing girl-boy-girl-boy-girl. All of them had long hair and bell-bottom jeans and love beads. The women all had flowers in their hair. The men had scruffy facial hair. The picture was old—I would guess that it'd been taken in the 1960s—and the five were probably college students or around that age. The image reminded me of stuff I'd seen in a Woodstock documentary.

The colors in the photograph had faded over the years, but you could tell that at one time they'd been bright. The five stood in front of a brick building and all smiled widely. They all wore the same tie-dyed T-shirts with a bizarre emblem on the chest. At first I thought it was some sort of peace sign. But no, that wasn't it. I looked closer, but I couldn't figure out what it was. The emblem looked like, I don't know, a messed-up butterfly maybe. I read once about Rorschach blots, where different people see different things in the same vague images. It was a little like that, except the blots were black while this design had a host of colors. I looked again. Yes, I could clearly make out a butterfly. Near the bottom tips of the wings, there were two round . . . eyes, I guess. Animal eyes maybe. They seemed to glow.

Seriously creepy.

My gaze kept being drawn back to the girl in the center of the picture. She stood a little forward, as though she were the leader. She had waist-length blond hair lassoed with a purple headband. Her T-shirt was, uh, snug, if you know what I mean, tight across a rather curvy figure. Just as I was thinking that this particular hippie chick was kind of hot, a horrible realization hit me:

It was Bat Lady.

Ugh!

When my phone vibrated, I jumped again. I quickly pulled it into view and looked at the message. It was from Ema. The text was all in screaming caps: **CAR COMING! GET OUT!**

I put the photograph on the mantel and headed back toward the kitchen. I kept low, nearly commando-crawling on the dirty linoleum. When I reached the wall, I rose slowly and peeked out the window into the backyard. In the woods, the cloud of dirt settled.

I could see the car now.

It was pure black with tinted windows. A limousine or town car or something. It had stopped in front of Bat Lady's garage. I waited, not sure what to do. Then the passenger door opened.

For a moment, nothing happened. I glanced left, then right, looking for Ema. There she was, trying to hide behind a tree. Ema pointed to my right. Huh? I gave her a what-gives? shrug. She kept pointing, more insistent now. I looked in that direction.

The kitchen door was still open! I'd forgotten to close it.

I ducked low and stretched my leg toward it. Using my foot, I kicked the door closed, though it didn't stick. It popped back open, creaking in the still air. I tried again, but the lock was broken. The door wouldn't stay closed. I nudged it closed so that it was just ajar now.

I risked a glance back at the window. Ema glared at me and started working her cell phone. The message buzzed in: **what part of CAR COMING! GET OUT! confused u?!? HURRY, DOPE!**

I didn't move. Not yet. First of all, I wasn't sure which direction to go. I couldn't go out the back—whoever was in the black car would spot me. I could run out the front, but that might draw their attention too. So for now, I stayed put. I kept my eye on the car. And I waited.

The front passenger door of the car opened a little more. I stayed low, keeping only my forehead and eyes above the window line. I saw one shoe hit the dirt, then another. Black shoes. Men's. A moment later someone rose from the car.

Yep, a man. His head was shaved clean. He wore a dark suit and aviator sunglasses and looked as if he were either coming from a funeral or an elite member of the Secret Service.

Who the heck was this?

The man kept his body ramrod straight while his head spun like a robot's, scanning the area. He stopped on the tree where Ema was doing a pretty poor job of hiding. He took a step toward her. Ema squeezed her eyes shut, as though wishing herself away. The man with the shaved head took another step.

No doubt about it. He had seen her.

I debated what to do here—but not for very long. I had to act fast, had to distract him. I decided to hit the back door and draw his attention. I was about to do just that when Ema opened her eyes. She spun out from behind the tree, all in her black goth wear. The man stopped in his tracks.

"Yo," Ema said. "Would you like to buy some Girl Scout cookies?"

The man with the aviator sunglasses stared for a moment. Then he said, "You're trespassing."

His voice was flat, lifeless.

"Right, sorry about that," she said. "See, I was going around the neighborhood, and I was about to knock on your front door when I heard your car, so I figured, what the heck, I'd make it easier on you and come around back."

She tried to smile at him. He didn't seem pleased. Ema kept talking.

"Now, our most popular cookie is still the Thin Mint, but we recently introduced a new flavor, the Dulce de Leche, though I think they're too sweet, and if you're watching your calories—I know, it doesn't look like I do, am I right?—you can try our new Sugar-Free Chocolate Chip."

The man just stared at her.

"Or we still sell the Samoas, the Peanut Butter Sandwiches, the Shortbreads and the Tagalongs. I don't want to pressure sell, but all your neighbors have placed orders. The Asseltas next door? They bought thirty boxes, and with a little help I can land first place in my troop and win a hundred-dollar gift certificate to the American Girl doll store—"

"Go."

"I'm sorry. Did you say—"

"Go." There was no give in his voice. "Now."

"Right, okay." Ema raised her hands in mock surrender and quickly moved out of sight. I fell back for a second, relieved. I was also impressed as all get-out. Talk about quick thinking. Ema was safe. Now it was my turn. I took another glance out the window. The man with the shaved head stood by the garage door. He opened it, and whoever was driving pulled the car in. The man with the shaved head kept doing the head pivot, like a surveillance camera, and then suddenly he jerked to the left and zeroed right in on me.

I dropped back down to the floor, out of sight.

Had he spotted me? It seemed likely, the way he homed in on me like that, but with the sunglasses on, it was impossible to know. I crawled back to the other room, positioning myself on the floor so I could see the back door.

I had my cell phone in my hand. I quickly texted Ema: **U OK?**

Two seconds later Ema replied: **yes. GET OUT!**

She was right. Keeping low, I started across the kitchen floor. I passed the spiral staircase again. I thought about what might be up there and shuddered.

Who was that creepy dude with the shaved head and dark suit?

Maybe the explanation was simple, I thought. Maybe it was a relative of Bat Lady's. All dressed in black like that— maybe it was her nephew or something. Maybe he was Bat Nephew.

I was almost at the front door now. So far, no one had come in. Perfect. I stood up and took one more glance at the sixties photograph, at the weird butterfly emblem on all their T-shirts. I looked at the other faces, tried to take a mental picture so I could review it later. My hand found the knob.

And that was when a light came on behind me.

I froze.

The light was dim, but in this darkness . . . I slowly spun my head.

There was light coming from the crack beneath the basement door. Someone was in the basement—someone who had just this moment turned on the light down there.

A dozen thoughts hit me all at once. The biggest was a

one-word command: *RUN!* I had watched the horror movies, the ones where the mentally malnourished airhead goes into the house alone, sneaking around like, well, like me, and then ends up with an ax between the eyes. From the safety of my seat in the cineplex, I had scoffed at their idiocy and now, here I was, in Bat Lady's lair, and someone else was here, in the basement.

Why had I come?

It was simple really. Bat Lady had called me by my name. She had said that my father was alive. And while I knew that it couldn't possibly be true, I was willing to risk whatever, including my personal safety, if there was a chance, just the slightest chance, that there was an inkling of truth in what she said.

I missed my dad so much.

The basement door glowed. I knew the glow was my imagination or an optical illusion based on the fact that the light coming from the basement was bright while the rest of the house was so dark. That didn't help calm me down.

I stayed still and listened. Now I could hear someone moving down there. I moved closer to the door. There were voices. Two people. Both male.

My phone buzzed again. Ema: **GET! OUT!**

Part of me wanted to stay. Part of me wanted to fling open that basement door and take my chances. But another part of me—maybe the part of me that was millions of years old, the animal part, the primordial part that still relied on survival instinct—pulled up. The primordial animal looked at that glowing door and sensed danger behind it.

Serious danger.

I moved back to the front of the house. I turned the knob, opened the door, and ran.

chapter 4

I MET UP WITH EMA three blocks away.

"That," she said, cracking a smile for the first time since I'd known her, "was awesome."

"Yeah," I said. "I guess."

"So where do you want to break into next?"

"Funny." And then I couldn't help but smile.

"What?" she said.

I started laughing.

"What?"

"You," I said. "Selling Girl Scout cookies."

She laughed too. The sound was melodious. "What, you don't buy me as a Girl Scout?"

I just looked at her—in the black clothes, with the black nail polish and silver studs in her eyebrow. "Yeah, nice uniform."

"Maybe I'm the goth Girl Scout." She lifted up her cell phone to show me. "Oh, I typed in the license plate number of that black car. I don't know what you can do with it, but I figured what the heck."

I had an idea about that. "Can you text it to me?"

Ema nodded, typed a little, hit Send. "So what are you going to do now?" she asked.

I shrugged. What could I do? I couldn't call the police. What would I tell them? A man in a dark suit walked into a garage? For all I knew he lived there. And how would I explain to the police my being inside the house in the first place?

I told her about the photograph, the butterfly emblem, and the light in the basement. When I finished, Ema said, "Whoa."

"You say that a lot."

"What?"

"'Whoa,'" I said.

"Actually, I don't. But hanging around you, well, it seems awfully apropos."

I checked the time on my cell phone. It was time to meet Spoon so we could break into the main office. If I made it through today without going to jail, it would be a miracle.

"I have to go," I said.

"Thanks for the adventure."

"Thanks for being the lookout."

"Mickey?"

I turned and looked at her.

"What are you going to do about Bat Lady?"

"I don't know," I said. "What can I do?"

"She told you your dad is alive."

"Yeah, so?"

"We can't just let that go."

"We?"

Ema blinked and looked away. There were tears in her eyes.

"You okay?" I asked.

"Her saying that to you," Ema said. "It's so mean. We should egg her house—except then it would look and smell better." She wiped her face with the tattooed forearm. "I better go."

Ema started walking away.

"Wait, where do you live?" I asked. "Do you need me to walk you home?"

She frowned. "Are you for real? Walk me home? Yeah, right."

She hurried her step and vanished around the corner. I thought about chasing after her, but she'd dig into me about the fat girl needing protection and I didn't have time for that. Spoon was waiting for me.

I jogged back to the school and found him alone in the parking lot. I pushed away all images of the Bat Lady and her house. I was still riding the adrenaline wave—might as well see where it led me. Spoon was sitting on the hood of a car.

"Hey, Spoon."

"Guess what?" He jumped down from the hood. "Beyoncé's favorite makeup is mascara, but she's allergic to perfume."

He waited expectantly for me to reply.

"Uh, interesting," I said.

"I know, right?"

I should have nicknamed him Random instead of Spoon.

Spoon led the way toward the side door of the school. Using the card in his hand, he swiped it through the magnetic reader. There was a click, and the door opened. We entered.

There is no place more hollow, more soulless, than a school at night. The building had been created for life, for constant motion, for students rushing back and forth, some confident, most scared, all trying to figure out their place in the world. Take that away and you might as well have a body drained of all its blood.

Our footsteps in the long corridors echoed so loudly I wondered if our shoes were amped up. We headed for the main office without speaking. When we reached the glass door, Spoon had the key at the ready.

"If my dad finds out," Spoon whispered, "well, no revival of *Guys and Dolls* for me."

He looked back at me. I guess I should have given him an out here. But I didn't. Maybe because I was that desperate. Or maybe because I don't like *Guys and Dolls*. He turned the key, and we stepped into the office. The front desk was tall enough so you could lean on it. Three school secretaries sat there. Going behind the desk was, of course, strictly off-limits, so I confess that I got a thrill when we did just that.

Spoon took out a penlight. "It's darker in there. We can't turn on any lights, okay?"

I nodded.

We stopped at a door that read GUIDANCE. I always found that term wonderfully vague. The dictionary definition of the word is "advice or information aimed at resolving a problem." In short, an attempt to help. But to us students, the word—this office—is far more frightening. It conjures up our college prospects, growing older, getting a real job—our future.

Guidance seemed more like a term for cutting us loose.

Spoon fished out another key and opened the door. The school, I knew, had twelve guidance counselors. Each had a small private office within this larger office. Most of the doors were unlocked. We entered the first private office. It belonged to a young guidance counselor named Ms. Korty. Like most people, she had left her computer on for the night, settling for "standby" mode.

Spoon handed me the penlight and nodded for me to go ahead. I sat at her desk and started typing. As soon as I hit the keys, the following prompt popped up:

USER NAME:
PASSWORD:

Damn! I hit the return key several times. Nothing. I sighed and looked back at Spoon. "Do you have a clue?"

"The user name is easy," Spoon said. "It's just her e-mail. Janice Korty, so it's JKorty at the school dot e-d-u."

"And the password?"

Spoon pushed the glasses up his nose. "That's going to be a problem."

I tried to think. "How about paper files?"

"They're kept off-site. And if Ashley is a new student, she probably doesn't even have one yet."

I sat back, defeated. Then I let myself think about Ashley. My shoulders relaxed. I thought about the way she nervously played with a loose thread on her sweater. I thought about the way she smelled like wildflowers and when I kissed her, she tasted gently like berries. I know how corny this sounds, but I could kiss her all day and never get bored. Barf, right? I thought of the way she would look at me sometimes, like I was the only person in the universe, and then I thought that this girl, the one who looked at me like that, had just vanished without a good-bye.

It made no sense.

I had to think harder. Ms. Korty was young—the youngest guidance counselor at the school. Something about that triggered a thought. I turned to Spoon. "Who are some of the oldest guidance counselors?"

"Oldest? You mean, like age?"

"Yes."

"Why?"

"Humor me."

"Mr. Betz," Spoon said without hesitation. "He's so old he teaches a class on Shakespeare because he knew him personally."

I had seen Mr. Betz in the corridors. He used a walking stick and wore a bow tie. I thought about it—he could definitely be my man. "Which office is his?"

"Why?"

"Just show me, okay?"

When we got back into the hallway, Spoon pointed to the office in the far corner. As we headed toward it, I peered quickly into each office we passed, glancing at the computer monitors for Post-it Notes. No luck. Mr. Betz's desk had antique-globe bookends and a matching pen holder with his name engraved on it. There was an old Swingline stapler and several Lucite awards.

I sat at his desk and turned on the computer. The same prompt came up:

USER NAME:
PASSWORD:

Spoon looked at me and shrugged. "What did you expect?"

Exactly this. I opened the drawer on the right. Pens, pencils, paper clips, a box of matches, a pipe. I moved to the middle drawer. I looked inside, smiled, and said, "Bingo."

"Huh?"

While it never pays to generalize, those who appear not to be the most computer literate often rely on keeping old-fashioned notes so that they don't forget stuff like user names and passwords. There, on a classic three-by-five index card, Mr. Betz had written the following:

GLOBETHEATRE1599

If that wasn't a password . . .

Spoon said, "Shakespeare's Globe Theatre was originally built in 1599. It was destroyed by fire on June 29, 1613, and rebuilt in 1614 and closed in 1642. A modern reconstruction of it was opened in 1997."

Terrific. Mr. Betz's first name was Richard. I typed in the RBetz user name and typed GLOBETHEATRE1599 in as the password. I hit the return button and waited. A little hourglass spun for a second before a screen came up:

WELCOME, RICHARD!

Spoon smiled and held up a palm. I high-fived him. I clicked the link for student files and then typed in the name: Kent, Ashley. When her photograph came up—the one we'd both taken for student IDs the first day of school—I felt a hand reach into my chest and squeeze my heart.

"Man," Spoon said, "no wonder you want to find her."

If you were creating a graphic dictionary and needed a definition of *demure*, you would use her expression in this picture. She looked pretty, sure, beautiful even, but what you really felt was that she was quiet and shy and somewhat uncomfortable posing. Something about it—something about her, really—called out to me.

Her file was brief. Her parents were listed as Patrick and Catherine Kent. Their home phone and address on Carmenta Terrace were there. I grabbed a pen from Mr. Betz's holder and found a scrap of paper.

"Fingerprints," Spoon said, pointing to the pen. "For that matter, your fingerprints are probably on his keyboard."

I made a face. "You think they're going to dust for prints?"

"They might."

"Then I choose to live dangerously," I said.

I jotted down the address and phone. I scanned the rest of the page. It said: TRANSCRIPT PENDING. I guess that meant that they didn't have anything from her old school. There was a list of her current classes, but I already knew those. The rest of the screen was blank. I was tempted to check out my own file—just out of curiosity, I guess—but Spoon gave me a look to hurry. I carefully put the pen back in its place, pretended to wipe away all my prints, and followed Spoon out.

Once outside I checked my phone. Another voice mail from Uncle Myron. I ignored it. Darkness had fallen now.

I looked up at the stars in the ink-black sky. It was a clear night.

"Do you know where Carmenta Terrace is?" I asked Spoon.

"Sure. It's on my way home. Do you want me to take you?"

I said I did. And off we went.

Spoon was on my right, a good foot shorter than me. He watched his feet while he walked.

"In the morning," Spoon said, "I'm making waffles."

I smiled. "I know that one," I said.

"You do?"

"Donkey to Shrek."

"You play basketball," Spoon said.

I couldn't tell if it was a question or statement. I nodded. When you're six-four, you get used to that question.

"Your name is Mickey Bolitar," he said.

"Yep."

"The name Myron Bolitar is all over the gym. He holds almost every basketball record at the school. Most points, most rebounds, most wins."

As I knew only too well.

"Is he your father?" Spoon asked.

"My uncle."

"Oh." We kept walking. "The basketball team was eighteen and five last year," Spoon said. "They lost in the state finals. The top six players are all returning. They'll be seniors this year."

I knew all this. It was one of the reasons I, a lowly sophomore, was keeping my own game under wraps for the time being. I hadn't played in town yet, choosing instead to find more competitive pickup games in Newark.

We passed a football practice for kids who couldn't have been older than ten. The coaches screamed like it was Division I-A. This town was big on athletics. The first week of school I asked someone how many pro athletes had come out of this high school. The answer was one: my uncle. And in truth he never really played pro basketball. He was drafted in the first round but blew out his knee in preseason. *Boom*, like that, his career was over. Uncle Myron never got to suit up for the Celtics. I thought about that sometimes, about what that must have been like, and I wonder if that explained the tension between him and my dad.

But it was still Myron's fault—what happened between him and my dad. So I saw no reason to forgive.

"It's up this way," Spoon said.

The stone sign in front of what looked like a new development read THE PREMA ESTATES. The area reeked of new money. The streets were well lit. The lawns couldn't have been greener without using an industrial-strength spray paint. The landscaping was almost too polished, like a show that had over-rehearsed. The sprawling mansions were brick and stone, trying to look old and stately but missing.

When we hit the top of Carmenta Terrace, I looked out at the Kents' house and felt my heart drop.

Four police cars, all with spinning lights, were parked in front of it. Worse, there was an ambulance in the driveway. I broke into a run. Despite being a foot shorter, Spoon stayed with me stride for stride. There were police officers on the lawn. One was talking to what I assumed was a neighbor. The cop was taking notes. The front door of the Kent house was open. I could see a foyer and a big chandelier and a cop on guard.

When we reached the curb, Spoon pulled up. I didn't stop. I ran toward the door. The cop at the door turned, startled, and yelled, "Halt."

I did. "What happened?" I asked him.

Spoon came up next to me. The cop frowned his disapproval with everything he had. Not just his mouth frowned. All of him joined in. He had a unibrow and Cro-Magnon forehead. They frowned too. He glared at Spoon, then turned it back at me. "And you are?"

"I'm a friend of Ashley's," I said.

He crossed his arms over a chest that could have doubled as a paddleball court. "Did I ask you for a list of your friends?" he said with a gigantic sigh. "Or did I ask who you are?"

Oh boy. "My name is Mickey Bolitar."

That got the brow up in the air. "Hold up a second. You're Myron's kid?"

He said Myron's name like he was spitting something really foul out of his mouth. "No. His nephew. If you could just tell me—"

"Do I look like a librarian?" he snapped.

"Excuse me?"

"You know. A librarian. I mean, do you think I'm here to answer your questions? Like a librarian."

I glanced at Spoon. He shrugged. I said, "No. No, I don't think you're a librarian."

"You being a wise guy?"

"Me? No."

He shook his head. "Smart mouth. Just like your uncle."

I was tempted to tell him that I didn't like my uncle either. I figured that it would bond us, like pulling a thorn from his paw, but no matter what I felt about my uncle, I wasn't about to sell my family down the river to appease Mr. Cro-Magnon.

Spoon said, "Officer?"

He turned hard at him. "What?"

"You're being rude," Spoon said.

Oh boy.

"What did you say to me?"

"You're a civil servant. You're being rude."

Cro-Magnon pushed his chest so it was right up against

Spoon's face. Spoon did not step back. Cro-Magnon stared down at him and then narrowed his eyes. "Wait a second. I know you. You were picked up last year, weren't you? Twice."

"And released," Spoon said. "Twice."

"Yeah, I remember. Your father wanted to sue us for false arrest or some crap like that. You're that old janitor's kid, right?"

"I am."

"So," Cro-Magnon said with a sneer, "does your dad still clean toilets for a living?"

"Sure, that's his job," Spoon said, pushing up his glasses. "Toilets, sinks, floors—whatever needs cleaning."

The guilelessness threw him. I quickly stepped in. "Look, we aren't looking to cause any trouble. I just want to make sure my friend is okay."

"Big hero," he said, turning back to me. I saw now that he wore a name tag—TAYLOR. "Like your uncle." Taylor made a big production of putting his hands on his hips. "Strange you two being out so late on a school night."

I tried not to make a face. "It's eight o'clock."

"You being a wise guy again?"

I needed to get past this guy.

"Maybe you two should come with me."

"Where?" I asked.

Taylor put his face so close to mine I could bite his nose. "How about a holding cell, smart guy? You like that idea?"

Spoon said, "No."

"Well, that's where you're heading if you don't start answering my questions. There's this one we got down in Newark I think will be perfect for you two. I can put you in separate cells. Adult population. One guy we have in holding right now, he's seven feet tall and got these really long fingernails because, well, he likes to scratch things."

He grinned at us.

Spoon swallowed hard. "You can't do that," he said.

"Aw, you gonna cry?"

"We're minors," Spoon said. "If you arrest us, you need to contact our parents or guardian."

"Can't," Taylor said with a smirk. "Your daddy is too busy scrubbing toilets with his brush."

"He doesn't use a brush," Spoon said. "He uses your mama's face."

Oh boy.

Something behind Taylor's eyes exploded. His face went scarlet red. I thought that maybe he was having a stroke. His hands formed fists. Spoon stood right there. He pushed his glasses back up his nose. I thought that Taylor was going to punch him. Maybe he would have, but a voice yelled, "Out of the way, coming through."

A stretcher was heading toward us. We stepped to either side of the door. A man was on it. There were contusions on his face, but he was conscious. A few spots of blood clung to the collar of his white dress shirt. I would guess his age as early forties. Ashley's father? A woman about the same age trailed him. Her face was ghost pale. She clutched her purse as though it could offer comfort.

She stopped, dazed. "Who are these two?" she asked Taylor.

"We, uh, found them loitering around," Taylor said. "We thought maybe they were the perpetrators."

For a second, Mrs. Kent stared at us as though we were pieces in a puzzle she couldn't put together.

"These are boys," she said.

"Yes, I know, but—"

"I told you it was a man. I told you he had a tattoo on his face. Do you see a tattoo on either of their faces?"

Taylor said, "I was just eliminating . . ." But she was already gone, catching up to the stretcher. Taylor shot another glare toward us. Spoon actually gave him a thumbs-up, as though he'd done a good job. Again, with that facial expression, you couldn't tell if Spoon was goofing on him or sincere. Based on the mama line, I assumed the former.

"Get out of here," Taylor said.

We headed back down the brick walk. The man I assumed was Ashley's father was loaded into the back of the ambulance. A police officer was talking to Mrs. Kent. Two other cops were talking near us. I heard the words *home invasion* and felt my chest tighten.

Now or never.

I ran over before anyone could stop me. "Mrs. Kent?"

She stopped and frowned at me. "Who are you?"

"My name is Mickey Bolitar. I'm a friend of Ashley's."

She said nothing for a second. Her eyes shifted to the right, then back toward me. "What do you want?"

"I just want to make sure Ashley is okay."

When she shook her head, I felt my knees buckle. But then she said something I never expected: "Who?"

"Ashley," I said. "Your daughter."

"I don't have a daughter. And I don't know anyone named Ashley."

chapter 5

HER WORDS PARALYZED ME.

Mrs. Kent stepped into the back of the ambulance. The cops chased us away. When we reached the bottom of Prema Estates, Spoon and I split up and headed to our respective homes. I called the Coddington Rehab Center on my way, but they told me that my mother was in session and it was too late to talk or visit tonight. That was fine. She was coming home tomorrow morning anyway.

Uncle Myron's car, a Ford Taurus, was in the driveway. When I opened the front door, Myron called out, "Mickey?"

"Homework," I said, hurrying into my bedroom in the basement to avoid him. For many years, including his stint in high school, the basement had been Myron's bedroom. Nothing in it had changed since. The wood paneling was flimsy and stuck on with two-sided tape. There was a bean-bag chair that leaked small pellets. Faded posters of basketball greats from the 1970s, guys like John "Hondo" Havlicek and Walt "Clyde" Frazier, adorned the walls. I confess that I loved the posters. Most of the room was like lame retro. But nobody was cooler than Hondo and Clyde.

I did my math homework. I don't dislike math, but is there anything more boring than math homework? I read a little Oscar Wilde for English and practiced vocabulary for French. When I was done, I grilled myself a cheeseburger on the barbecue.

Had Mrs. Kent lied to me? And why?

I couldn't fathom a reason, which led immediately to the next question.

Had Ashley lied to me? And why?

I tried to run through the possibilities in my brain, but nothing came to me. With dinner over, I grabbed the basketball, flipped on the outdoor lights, and started to shoot. I play every day. I do my best thinking when I shoot hoops.

The court is my escape and my paradise.

I love basketball. I love the way you can be exhausted and sweaty and running with nine other guys, and yet, at the risk of sounding overly Zen, you are still so wonderfully alone. On the court, nothing bothers me. I see things a few seconds before they actually happen. I love anticipating a teammate's cut and then throwing a bounce pass between two defenders. I love the rebound, boxing out, figuring angles and positioning myself, willing the ball into my hands. I love dribbling without looking down, the feel, the sense of trust, of control, almost as though the ball were on a leash. I love catching the pass, locking my eyes on the front rim, sliding my fingers into the grooves, raising the ball above my head, cocking my wrist as I begin to leap. I love the feel as I release the shot at the apex of the jump, the way my fingertips stay on the leather until the last possible moment, the way I slowly come back to the ground, the way the ball moves in an arc toward the rim, the way the bottom of the net dances when the ball goes *swish*.

I moved now around the blacktop, taking shots, grabbing my own rebounds, moving to another spot. I played games in my head, pretending LeBron or Kobe or even Clyde and Hondo were covering me. I took foul shots, hearing the sportscaster in my head announcing that I, Mickey Bolitar, had two foul shots and my team was down by one and there was no time left on the clock and it was game seven of the NBA Finals.

I let myself get deliriously lost in the bliss.

I had been shooting for an hour when the back door opened. Uncle Myron came out. He didn't say a word. He moved under the basket and started grabbing rebounds and passing the ball back to me. I moved through the shots in around-the-world fashion, starting in the right corner and moving to my left, taking a shot every yard or so, until I ended up in the opposite corner.

Myron just rebounded for me. He got it, the need for silence right now. This, in a sense, was our church. We understood respect. So for a while he let it go. When I signaled that
I wanted to take a break, he spoke for the first time.

"Your father used to do this for me," Myron said. "I
would shoot. He would rebound."

My father had done the same for me too, but I didn't feel
like sharing that.

Myron's eyes welled up. They well up a lot. Myron was
overly emotional. He was always trying to raise the subject
of my father with me. We would drive past a Chinese restaurant and he'd say, "Your father loved the pork fried dump-
lings here," or we'd go past the Little League field and he'd
say, "I remember when your father hit a ground-rule double
when he was nine to win a game."

I never responded.

"One night," Myron went on, "your father and I played
a game of horse that went on for three hours. Think about
that. We finally agreed to call it a draw when we both had
H-O-R-S for thirty straight minutes. Thirty straight minutes.
You should have seen it."

"Sounds epic," I said in my flattest monotone.

Myron laughed. "God, you're a wiseass."

"No, no, a game of horse. You and Dad must have been
party animals."

Myron laughed some more and then we fell into silence. I
started for the door when he said, "Mickey?"

I turned toward him.

"I'll drive you and your mom tomorrow morning. Then I'll leave you two alone."

I nodded a thanks.

Myron grabbed the basketball and started shooting. It was his escape too. Not long ago, I found an old clip of his injury on YouTube. Myron was wearing a Boston Celtics jersey with the horrible short-shorts they wore in those days. He'd been pivoting on his right leg when Burt Wesson, a bruiser on the Washington Bullets, slammed into him. Myron's leg bent in a way it was never supposed to. You could hear the snap even in the old video.

I watched him another second or two, noticing the startling similarities in the release on our jump shots. I started to go back into the house when a thought made me pause. After his injury Myron became a sports agent. That's how my parents met—Myron was going to represent the teen tennis sensation Kitty Hammer, aka my mother. Eventually Myron branched out to represent not just athletes but people in the arts, theater, and music. He even repped rock star Lex Ryder, half of the duo that made up the group HorsePower.

Mom had known HorsePower. So had Dad. Myron represented them. And Bat Lady had their first album, which had to be thirty years old now, on her turntable.

I turned back to Myron. He stopped shooting and looked back at me. "What's wrong?"

"Do you know anything about the Bat Lady?" I asked.

He frowned. "The old house on the corner of Pine and Hobart Gap?"

"Yes."

"Wow. Bat Lady. She has to be long dead."

"What makes you say that?"

"I don't know. I can't believe kids still make up stories about her."

"What kind of stories?"

"She was like the town bogeyman," he said. "Supposedly she kidnapped children. People claimed they saw her bringing children to her house late at night, stuff like that."

"Did you ever see her?" I asked.

"Me? No." Myron spun the ball on his fingers, staring at it a little too intently. "But I think your father did."

I wondered if this was yet another attempt by Myron to bring up my father, but no, that didn't seem to be Myron's style. He was a lot of things, my uncle, but he wasn't a liar.

"Can you tell me about it?"

I could see that Myron wanted to ask why, but he also didn't want to ruin the moment. I didn't talk to him much and never about my dad. He didn't want to risk me clamming back up. "I'm trying to think," he said, rubbing his chin. "Your dad must have been twelve, maybe thirteen, I don't remember. Anyway, we walked past that house our whole lives. You know the stories about it already, and you've lived here only a few weeks. So you can imagine. One time, your father and I, we were young then, he was maybe seven, I was twelve or so, we went to a horror movie at the Colony and we decided to walk back. It got dark and started to rain and we walked past some older kids. They chased us and started yelling how the Bat Lady was going to get us. Your father was so scared he started to cry."

Myron stopped and looked off. He was fighting off tears again.

"After that night, your dad was always afraid of the Bat Lady's house. I mean, like I said, we were all creeped out, but your father didn't even want to walk past it. He had nightmares about the house. I remember he went to a sleepover party and he woke up screaming about the Bat Lady coming to get him. The kids teased him about it. You know how it is."

I nodded that I did.

"So one Friday night, Brad is out with friends. That's what we used to do back then. We'd just hang out at night. So anyway, it's getting dark and they're bored, so one thing leads to another and the friends challenge Brad to knock on Bat Lady's door. He doesn't want to, but your father was not one to lose face."

"So what happened next?"

"He approached Bat Lady's house. It was pitch dark. No lights were on. His friends stayed across the street. They figured he'd knock and then run. Well, he knocked, but he didn't run. His friends all waited to see if Bat Lady answered the door. But that's not what happened. Instead they saw your father turn the knob and go inside."

I almost gasped. "On his own?"

"Yep. He disappeared inside, and his friends waited for him to come out. They waited a long time. But he didn't come back. After a while, they figured that Brad was playing a trick on them. You know. The house was empty, so all Brad did was sneak out the back—trying to scare them by not coming out."

I took a step closer to Myron. "So what did happen?"

"One of your dad's old friends, Alan Bender, well, he didn't buy that. So when your dad didn't show up for two hours, he was terrified. He ran to our house to get help or at least tell someone. I remember he was out of breath and all wide eyed. I was out back here shooting, just like, well, tonight. Alan told me that he saw Brad go into Bat Lady's house and that he didn't come out."

"Were Grandma and Grandpa home?"

"No, they were out to dinner. It was a Friday night. We didn't have cell phones back then. So I ran back with Alan. I started pounding on Bat Lady's door, but there was no answer. Alan said that he saw your dad just turn the knob and walk in. So I tried that, but the door was locked now. From inside, I thought I could hear music playing."

"Music?"

"Yeah. It was weird. I started freaking out. I tried to kick in the door, if you could believe it, but it held. I told Alan to run to the neighbor's house and have them call the police. So Alan takes off. And just as he does, the front door opens and your father walks out. Just like that. He looks so serene. I ask him if he's okay. He says, sure, fine."

"What else did he say?"

"That's it."

"Didn't you ask him what he'd been doing for two hours?"

"Of course."

"And?"

"He never said."

The hairs on the back of my neck stood up. "Never?"

Myron shook his head. "Never. But something happened. Something big."

"What do you mean?"

"He was different after that, your father."

"How?"

"I don't know. More thoughtful maybe. More mature. I thought it was just because he faced his fears. But maybe there was more to it than that. A few weeks ago, Grandpa told me that he always knew your dad would run off—that he was meant to be a nomad. I never quite bought that. But I think that started, that feeling that your dad was meant to wander, after he visited the Bat Lady's house."

chapter 6

SLEEP DIDN'T COME easily that night.

I thought about Bat Lady. I thought about Ashley. But mostly I thought about my mother coming home in the morning. At seven A.M., Myron drove me to the Coddington Rehabilitation Institute. The drive was only about ten minutes, but it felt ten times longer. When we arrived, I jumped out of the car before it even came to a stop. Myron called out to me that he'd wait out here. I waved thanks in mid-sprint.

The security guard nodded and called me by name as I flew by him. Everyone here knows me. I visit my mother every day, except when their protocol doesn't allow it.

Christine Shippee owned the place, but she also liked to work the front desk. Her facial expression was permanently set on grumpy, peering intensely at everyone through a Plexiglas window. I nodded at her and rushed through a lobby that reminded me of a fancy hotel. I stopped at the entrance so she could buzz me right in. She didn't. I walked over to where she sat.

She studied me for a moment. "Good morning, Mickey."

"Good morning, Mrs. Shippee."

"Big day," Christine said.

"Yep."

"I've warned you all about the pitfalls."

"You have."

"And I've told you how the chances of relapse are somewhat high."

"Several times."

"Super." Christine Shippee looked at me over her reading glasses. "Then there's no need to repeat myself."

"None."

She gestured with her head toward the door. "Go. Your mother is waiting."

I tried not to break into a sprint again, instead doing a little gallop down the corridor. When I entered her room and saw my mother, I broke into a smile. She looked great. For the past six weeks, she had been locked up in this place, detoxing, doing both group and individual therapy, taking pensive walks, exercising, eating right.

The day before Myron brought her here, my mother had gone out late to a seedy bar to get a fix. I used my fake ID—yes, I have a very good one—to get into the bar. I found her with a skuzzy guy, both half passed out, looking like something a cat had spit up.

Now the poison was out of her system. She looked like, well, my mom again.

Kitty—she wanted me to call her that for some reason, but I never did—hugged me and then she took my face in her hands. "I love you so much," she said.

"I love you too."

She winked and gestured to the door. "Let's get out of here before they change their minds."

"Good idea."

My mom was Kitty Hammer, and as I implied before, if that name rings a bell, you're probably a big-time tennis fan. When she was sixteen, Kitty Hammer was the number-one-ranked junior tennis player in the country. Mom was on track to be the next Venus or Billie Jean or Steffi, except something derailed her career for good:

She got pregnant with yours truly.

The world wasn't ready for my parents' relationship, I guess, so they ran off to parts unknown. Everyone predicted that the marriage would not last. Everyone was wrong. My mom and dad lived the corniest of love stories, and as I got older, it embarrassed me to no end. It was the kind of love that makes people jealous—and makes them cringe.

I used to want that kind of love for myself one day. Who doesn't, right? But I don't anymore. The problem with an all-consuming love like theirs is what happens when you lose it. Love like theirs turns two into one—so when my dad died, it was like ripping one entity in half, destroying my mom too. When we buried my father, I watched her crumble, like a puppet with its strings cut, and there was nothing I could do.

I learned a lesson from all this: that kind of obsessive storybook love was not for me. The end price was simply too high. While I liked Ashley a lot—while I cared about her and enjoyed my time with her—I would never let her or any girl get too close. Maybe she sensed that. Maybe that was why she ran away and never told me. Maybe that was why I should stop looking for her.

Uncle Myron was waiting for us next to his car. I tensed up as we approached. To say that the relationship between my mother and Myron was strained would be a gross under-statement. They pretty much hated each other. It was Myron, six weeks ago, who had threatened to take me away from her if she didn't agree to intensive rehabilitation.

I was surprised then when she walked up to him and gen-tly kissed him on the cheek. "Thank you."

He nodded, said nothing.

My mother has always been frighteningly honest with me. She was barely seventeen when she got pregnant with me, my dad nineteen. Myron thought that she had trapped my father. Myron called her names, even telling my dad that the baby—me—probably wasn't even his. It culminated in a fight between the two brothers that ripped them apart in a way that meant they would never be brought back together.

I know all this because my mother told me. She never forgave Myron for what he said about her. But here Mom was, fresh out of rehab, letting go of the past, surprising him, surprising me, and maybe that was the best sign of all.

As promised, Uncle Myron just dropped us off and left. "I'll be at the office if you need anything," he said. "The spare car is in the garage if you need one."

"Thank you," Mom said. "Thank you for everything."

Myron had converted the ground-level office into a bedroom for my mother. I would be in the basement below while Myron had the master bedroom upstairs. Most nights, before I came into his life, Myron stayed in a famous apartment building in Manhattan. My hope was, now that my mother was home, he'd go back to that routine and give us some privacy until we could get on our feet and find a place of our own.

Mom practically skipped into her room. When she saw the clothes laid out on the bed, she turned to me with a smile and said, "What's this?"

"I just bought you a few things."

It was nothing much. Some jeans and tops from a discount department store. Just enough to get her started. She came over and hugged me. "You know something?" she said to me.

"What?"

"We're going to be okay."

I flashed back to when I was twelve. Mom, Dad, and I were spending three months in Ghana. They did charity work for the Abeona Shelter, a group that specialized in feeding and caring for poor and at-risk children. My father often left us for two or three days at a time, doing missions in even more remote areas. One night when he was gone, I woke up with chills and a spiked fever. I felt so awful that I thought I was going to die. My mother rushed me to the hospital. It turned out I had malaria. I was woozy and dazed and sure that I wasn't going to make it. For three days, Mom never left my side. She held my hand and kept telling me that I was going to be okay, and it was her tone that made me believe it.

I heard that tone again now.

"I'm so sorry," Mom said.

"It's fine," I said.

"What I did. What I became . . ."

"It's behind us."

Here was what she didn't get: Mom had taken care of me my whole life. It was okay for it to be my turn for a while.

She started unpacking, humming while she did. She asked me about school and basketball. I gave her only the basics. I didn't want to worry her, so I didn't tell her about Ashley or especially about Bat Lady and what she'd said about Dad being alive. Don't get me wrong, I wanted to share all that with her. Like I said before, my mother was ridiculously open. But it wasn't the kind of thing you told someone the day she leaves rehab. It could wait.

My phone buzzed. I looked down at the incoming call. It

was Spoon, his third call this morning. Mom said, "Why don't you get that?"

"It's just someone from school."

That pleased her. "A new friend?"

"I guess."

"Don't be rude, Mickey. Answer it."

So I did, stepping into the hallway. "Hello?"

"Only male turkeys gobble," Spoon said. "Female turkeys make more of a clicking sound."

For this he called three times? Oh boy. "Great, Spoon, but I'm kind of busy."

"We forgot about Ashley's locker," Spoon said.

I switched hands. "What about it?"

"She had a locker here, right?"

"Right."

"Maybe there's a clue in it."

Genius, I thought. But I didn't want to leave Mom alone. "Let me call you back," I said, and pressed End.

When I came back in the room, Mom said, "What was that about?"

"Just something going on at school."

"What?"

"It's not important."

She looked at her watch. It was eight thirty. "You're going to be late."

"I thought I'd stay with you today," I said.

Mom arched an eyebrow. "And miss school? Oh, I don't think so. Don't worry. I've got a lot to do. I need to buy some more clothes. I need to go food shopping so I can make us dinner. I need to go back to Coddington for outpatient therapy in the afternoon. Come on, I'll drive you."

There was no room for protest, so I grabbed my backpack. Mom played the pop station and sang along softly. Normally her singing, off-key and enthusiastic as it was, made me roll my eyes. Not today. I sat next to her, closed my eyes, and just listened.

For the first time in so long, I let myself feel hope. This woman driving me to school was my mom. The junkie we had dropped off six weeks ago wasn't. That's what they don't tell you. The drugs didn't just change her. They stole her away, made her into something she wasn't.

We stopped in front of the school. I didn't want to leave her. She told me again not to worry.

"I'm going to the supermarket right now," she said. "Then I'm going to prepare us the absolute best dinner in the history of the world."

Mom was a great cook. She had learned how to prepare all kinds of exotic dishes during our years in exotic lands. "What are you making?"

She leaned in conspiratorially. "Spaghetti and meatballs."

Man, that sounded great. Talk about a perfect choice. Mom's spaghetti and meatballs, as she well knew, were my favorite. Pure comfort food. She took my face in both of her hands. She always did that, held my face. "I love you so much, Mickey."

I almost cried right then and there. "I love you too, Mom."

I started to get out of the car but she put a hand on my forearm.

"Wait." She fumbled for something in her purse. "You'll need a note, right? For being late?" She jotted one down. When I got out of the car, she drove off, smiling and waving. Anybody watching would think that she was just another mom dropping her kid at school.

chapter 7

I FOUND SPOON right before lunch.

"Look at this," he said.

He handed me an article he'd printed out. I figured that it would be on turkey sounds or Beyoncé, but no, it was a small piece on last night's "attempted robbery" at the Kent home. According to the police, a man had broken in and started ransacking the house when he realized that Mr. Kent was home. The intruder assaulted him but ran off when Mrs. Kent arrived. Mr. Kent's injuries were minor. He had been released from the hospital. The investigation was ongoing.

I still didn't get it. Did the Kents have a daughter or not? Maybe it would pay to visit the house again.

"Which way to her locker?" Spoon asked.

I showed him. As we walked, Spoon got his key ready.

"I'll need to do this fast," he said. "You block the line of vision. I don't want everyone seeing that I can open their lockers."

I nodded my agreement. But when we turned the corner and approached Ashley's locker, I could see right away that something was wrong. Spoon stopped and looked up at me.

Ashley's lock had been smashed open.

I wasn't sure what to do. Students were passing us by, oblivious, rushing to lunch or another class. I reached to open the locker and see what was inside when I felt eyes upon me. I turned and felt the quiet *boom* from her eyes.

It was Rachel Caldwell.

This won't sound like an earth-shattering pronouncement, but boys get funny around really hot girls. Rachel could tell the lamest jokes and boys fall about the place in laughter. She could offer the smallest smile and fill a boy's head with dreams that would last deep into nightfall. I would like to think I was above such things. For all I knew, Rachel had the brains of banana bread. But for a moment I met her gaze and felt my throat go dry.

Rachel stepped toward us. "Hi," she said.

Spoon licked his hand, patted down his cowlick, and gave Rachel the eye. "Did you know," he said to her, "that an octopus can't give you rabies?"

Rachel smiled at that. "You're cute."

Spoon swooned and almost fell backward.

She turned and met my eye again. "What are you doing?"

I shrugged and said the first thing I would ever say to Rachel Caldwell, School Hottie: "Uh, nothing."

The Return of Mr. Smooth.

Rachel looked at me again and then at the locker. For a moment I thought that she'd say more. But instead she gave the locker one last look and walked down the hallway. We watched her walk away. Rachel had some kind of walk.

"Put your tongues back in your mouths."

It was Ema.

"Hi," I said.

"Men," Ema said, shaking her head. "Or should I say, boys."

Spoon turned and stared at Ema.

She frowned at him. "What's your problem?"

Spoon licked his hand, patted down his cowlick, and gave her the eye. "Did you know," he said to her, "that an octopus can't give you rabies?"

"Creep."

Spoon shrugged at me. "It worked once. I figured . . ."

"I got it," I said.

"What are you two doing?" she asked.

I didn't bother answering. Instead I opened the locker. No surprise. It was empty. The bell rang, making us officially late for lunch. We hurried toward the cafeteria. I got in line. Spoon excused himself. I got two slices of pepperoni pizza and an apple—dairy, meat, fruit, bread, and if you counted tomato sauce, a vegetable. I moved to the table where Ema was sitting alone.

"Bolitar!"

I looked across the room to see who'd shouted my name. It was Buck and Troy. They glared at me and mashed their fists into their palms.

"I know," I said to them. "Dead man."

I put my tray next to Ema's. Two days in a row. That got some tongues wagging. Ema unwrapped the plastic from her sandwich and said, "So what was all that with the locker?"

I was about to answer when I heard someone making kissing noises in our direction. I turned and saw Buck and Troy, both still wearing their heavy varsity jackets. It had to be eighty degrees in here. I wondered if they slept in them.

"Awww," Buck said, "isn't this romantic?"

"Yeah," Troy added. "Two lovebirds sitting all by themselves."

They made more kissy noises. I looked at Ema. She just shrugged.

Buck: "You gonna start kissing now, lovebirds?"

Troy: "Yeah, you gonna start making out in the lunchroom?"

"No," I said, "we'll leave that to you two."

Buck and Troy turned chili-pepper red. Ema suppressed a smile. Buck opened his mouth but I held up a hand to stop him. "I know," I said. "Dead man."

"You don't know nothing," Troy spat. "You think you're so cool, right? Well, you're not."

"Good to know," I said.

Buck joined in. "You're new here, so we'll clue you in. You're sitting with a loser."

Troy said, "Yeah, a loser."

I took a bite of pizza.

Buck again: "Did she tell you how she got her nickname?"

I glanced at Ema. She nodded for me to let him keep going.

"See, one day, right, she was acting all emo in Spanish class, okay, and she's a chick, a fugly one, but a chick—"

I was about to get up, but Ema just shook her head.

"—right, not a guy, so, so we, one of us, actually I think it was Troy, right, Troy, it was you?"

"Yeah, right, Buck." Troy swelled with pride. "It was me."

They were both giggling now.

"So Troy says, just like this, no thought or nothing, just off the cuff, in the middle of class, Troy says, 'That fugly's not emo, she's Ema.' Get it?"

I said, "I get it."

"Because, see, we're in Spanish class with all the *a*'s and *o*'s at the end, and Troy just comes up with this name, Ema, just like that, and *boom*, it stuck. You see?"

I nodded. "You guys are the balls."

Spoon appeared. He put his tray on the other side of Ema's. Buck and Troy couldn't believe their luck. "Oh man, you're sitting here too?" Buck said. He pretended to jam a flag into the ground. "I declare this table Loserville."

More giggling.

"Loserville, USA," Troy said.

"USA," I said. "In case, what, we don't know what country we're in?"

I was about to get up again, but Ema put a hand on my forearm. "Hey, Buck," Ema said, "why don't you tell Mickey how you got the nickname 'Wee Wee Pants'?"

"What? That was never my nickname!"

"Sure it was. Troy, you probably never heard this one either, but it's absolutely true. See, when Buck was in fourth grade, he went to a birthday party at my house—"

"I've never been to your house! I don't even know where you live!"

"And Bucky had a little accident—"

"That's not true!"

Troy looked at Buck funny now. "Dude?"

"She's lying, Troy! Take it back, you dumb b—"

Ms. Owens appeared. "Is there a problem here?"

Everyone went silent. There were a bunch of "No, Ms. Owens" and then Buck and Troy faded away. I looked over at Ema. "Wee Wee Pants?"

Ema shrugged. "I just totally made that up."

Oh man, did I love this girl. "Really? So the part about a birthday party . . . ?"

"Made it up. The whole thing."

We bumped fists.

Spoon said, "Would you like to know a few fun facts about Troy?"

I took a bite of pizza. "Sure."

"Troy is a senior. He is captain of the boys' basketball team."

Terrific, I thought.

"But the most interesting fact about Troy is his last name."

"Which is?"

Spoon smiled. "Taylor."

I stopped mid-bite. "Taylor?"

"Yup."

"As in that cop who hassled us last night?"

"That was his dad," Spoon said. "He's actually the police chief here. In charge of the entire department."

Double terrific.

chapter 8

I WORRIED ABOUT MY MOM all day.

We exchanged a few just-checking-in-type texts. She seemed
upbeat. When the final bell rang, I found a quiet corner outside and called her cell phone. She answered on the third ring.
"Hi, Mickey."

I heard a little song in her voice and immediately relaxed.
"Where are you?"

"I'm back at the house," she said, "making you dinner."

"Everything is okay?"

"Everything is great, honey. I went to the supermarket. I
shopped for clothes at the mall. I even had a pretzel at the
food court. That might sound boring, but it was a wonderful day."

"I'm glad."

"How was school?"

"Good," I said. "So what do you want to do this afternoon?"

"I have outpatient therapy from four to five, remember?"

"Right."

"And don't you normally take the bus to basketball today?"

I had my steady pickup game in Newark. "I usually do."

"So?"

"So I thought I'd skip it today."

"Don't change your plans because of me, Mickey. You go play, and I'll go to therapy. By the time you get home, I'll have the spaghetti and meatballs ready. Oh, and I'm making homemade garlic bread too." Another one of my favorites—my mouth was already watering. "Will you be home by six?" she asked.

"Yes."

"Great. I love you, Mickey."

I told her I loved her too and then we hung up.

The bus station is on Northvale Avenue, half a mile from the school. Most of the commuters heading back to Newark at this hour are exhausted housekeepers trekking back to their urban dwellings after a day in the wealthier suburbs. They gave me strange looks, wondering what this white boy was doing on the bus with them.

The well-to-do grassy environs of Kasselton were only seven miles from the gritty streets of Newark, but the two cities seemed to be from different planets. I'm told that Newark is on the mend and while I see pockets of it, I mostly see the old decay. Poverty is still prevalent, but I go where the best basketball is and while you could talk prejudice or racial profiling, I'm still one of the very few white guys down here after school.

The two courts were made of cracked asphalt. The rims were rusted with metal rather than nylon nets. The backboard had dints and dings. I started coming down here about a month ago. Naturally I was greeted with skepticism, but that's the wonderful thing about basketball: you got game or you don't. At the risk of sounding immodest, I got game. I still get funny looks from the regulars, still get new-guy challenges, but that was something I thrived upon.

We were midway through the fifth game when I was stopped in my tracks by something I saw.

Earlier, we had chosen up sides. We play full court, five-on-five, "winners stay on, losers sit." That gives the game high stakes. No one wants to sit. The closest thing I have to a friend down here is Tyrell Waters, a junior point guard at nearby Weequahic High School. He's probably the only guy I've met here I feel comfortable with—mainly because we don't talk all that much. We just play.

Tyrell startled a few of the regulars by picking me first. Our team won the first four games in pretty easy fashion. For the fifth game, some of the guys on the sidelines tried to stack the sides so we would have stiffer competition. I loved the matchup.

But it was during that fifth game that I lost my focus a bit. These pickup games draw a surprisingly large and diverse crowd. Local toughs—Tyrell tells me that many are hardened gang members—hung off in the distance and glared. On the right, there was always a group of homeless men who cheered and jeered like real fans, applauding and booing and betting bottles of booze on the outcome. Closer in, leaning against the fence with stoic faces was a mix of local coaches, involved fathers, skuzzy agent wannabes, scouts from prep schools and even colleges. At least one guy, usually more, filmed the games for the purpose of recruitment.

So for a second, when we were coming back on defense, I glanced over at the crowd behind that fence. On the far right was the scout who recruited for an athletically high-powered parochial school. He approached me the other day, but I wasn't interested. Next to him was Tyrell's father, an investigator in the Essex County prosecutor's office, who loved to talk hoops and sometimes took Tyrell and me for milk shakes after the games. And next to him, third in from the right, standing there with sunglasses and a dark business suit, was the guy with the shaved head I'd seen at Bat Lady's house.

I froze.

"Mickey?" It was Tyrell. He had the ball and was heading downcourt. He looked at me, puzzled. "Come on, man."

I jogged after him, moving down to the low post. The score was 5–4, our lead. We play first team to ten by ones.

No one calls fouls—you just dealt with the contact and gave it back. I wanted to walk off the court right then and there, but you just didn't do that in pickup games. I glanced back over by the fence. The man was still wearing the aviator sunglasses, so I couldn't see his eyes, but I had no doubt where he was looking.

Directly at me.

I set up on the post and called for the ball. The guy covering me was six-eight and burly. We jockeyed for position, but I knew I had to end this game quickly, before the man from Bat Lady's house disappeared. I became a man possessed. I got the ball and drove down the middle, tossing up a baby hook over the front rim and in.

The man from Bat Lady's house watched in silence.

I turned it up a gear, scoring the next three baskets. Three minutes later, with my team up 9–4 now, Tyrell hit me on the left block. I pump-faked, spun to my left, and nailed a fade-away banker over the outstretched hand of a guy who was nearly seven feet tall. The crowd went "ooo" when the ball fell through the hoop. Game over. Tyrell offered me a fist bump and I took it on the run.

"Some shot," Tyrell said.

"Some pass," I countered, heading off the court.

"Hey," Tyrell said, "where you going?"

"I got to sit this one out," I said.

"You kidding? It's last game. We got a chance of sweeping."

He knew something had to be wrong. I never sat out.

The man from Bat Lady's house stood with the crowd behind the fence. When he saw me coming, he started to slide back and away. I didn't want to call out, not yet anyway, so I picked up my pace. Because of the fence, I had to circle around to get to him.

Tyrell came running up behind me. "What's wrong?"

"Nothing. I'll be right back."

I didn't want to break into a sprint. That would look too weird, so instead I did one of those fast-walk things. When I got around the fence, the homeless guys surrounded me, offering me high fives, encouragement, and of course, advice:

"You need to work on your left, man . . ."

"The drop step. Use that, see, and go baseline . . ."

"You gotta stick your butt out more on the box out. Like this . . ."

It was hard to rush through without being overtly rude, but now the man from Bat Lady's house was almost to the street corner, moving unhurriedly but somehow fast.

I didn't want to lose him.

"Wait!" I shouted.

He kept walking. I called out to him again. He stopped, turned, and for a second, I thought I saw the hint of a smile on his face. The heck with it. I pulled away from my wino fan base and dashed toward him. Heads turned from the suddenness of my movement. In the corner of my eye, I saw Tyrell's father notice what was going on and follow me.

The man from Bat Lady's house was across the street now, but I was closing the gap pretty quickly. I was maybe thirty, forty yards away from him when the black car with the tinted windows pulled up next to him.

"Stop!"

But I wasn't going to make it. The man paused and gave me half a nod, as if to say, *Nice try*. Then he slid into the passenger seat and before I could do anything, the car sped out of sight.

I didn't bother to take down the license plate. I already had it.

Tyrell's father, Mr. Waters, caught up. He looked at me with concern. "You okay, Mickey?"

"I'm fine," I said.

He wasn't buying it. "Do you want to tell me what that was about, son?"

Tyrell was there too now, standing next to his father. The two of them looked at me, together, side by side, shoulder to shoulder, and I hated myself for feeling such envy. I was grateful to this man for worrying about me, but I couldn't help but wish it were my own father standing here, concerned about my welfare.

"I just thought I recognized him, that's all," I said.

Tyrell's father still wasn't buying.

Tyrell said, "We still got one more game to play."

I thought about my mother heading back home after therapy, making the spaghetti and meatballs. I could almost smell the garlic bread. "It's getting late," I said. "I have to catch the bus back."

"I can drive you," Tyrell's father said.

"Thank you, Mr. Waters, but I can't ask you to go out of your way like that."

"It's no trouble. I got a case in Kasselton anyway. It'll be nice to have the company."

We lost the last game, in part because I was so distracted. When it was over, we all high-fived or fist-bumped good game. Mr. Waters waited for us. I took the backseat, Tyrell sat up front. He dropped Tyrell off at the two-family house they shared with Mr. Waters's sister and her two sons on Pomona Avenue, a tree-lined street in Newark's Weequahic section.

"You going to come down tomorrow?" Tyrell asked me.

I had been blocking on it, but now I remembered that Mom, Myron, and I were flying out in the morning to visit my father's grave in Los Angeles. It was a trip I didn't want to make; it was a trip I really needed to make.

"Not tomorrow, no," I said.

"Too bad," Tyrell said. "Fun games today."

"Yeah. Thanks for picking me."

"I just pick to win," he said with a smile.

Before he got out, Tyrell leaned over and kissed his father good-bye on the cheek. I felt another pang. Mr. Waters told his son to make sure he did his homework. Tyrell said, "Yes,

Dad," in an exasperated tone I remember using myself in better days. I moved up to the front passenger seat.

"So," Mr. Waters said to me as we hit Interstate 80, "what was with that bald guy in the black car?"

I didn't even know where to start. I didn't want to lie, but didn't know how to explain it. I couldn't tell him I'd broken into a house or any of that.

Finally I said, "He may be following me."

"Who is he?"

"I don't know."

"No idea at all?"

"None," I said.

Mr. Waters mulled that over. "You know that I'm a county investigator, right, Mickey?"

"Yes, sir. Is that like a cop?"

"That's exactly what it's like," he said. "And I was standing next to that guy the whole time you were playing. I'd never seen him down here before. He barely moved, you know? The whole time, he just stood there in that suit. Didn't cheer. Didn't call out. He never said a word. And he never took his eyes off you."

I wondered how he could tell that, what with the sunglasses and all, but I knew what he meant. We fell into silence for a moment or two. Then he said something that surprised me. "So while you guys played that last game, I took the liberty of running the guy's license plate."

"You mean on that black car?"

"Yes."

I sat perfectly still.

"It didn't come up in the system," he said.

"What does that mean?"

"It's classified."

"You mean like it's diplomatic or something?"

"Or something," he said.

I tried to put it together but nothing was coming to me. "So what does that mean exactly?"

We pulled up to Myron's house. He coasted to a stop and then turned to me. "The truth? I don't know, Mickey. But it doesn't sound good. Just please be careful, okay?"

"Okay," I said.

Mr. Waters reached into his wallet. "If you see that bald guy again, don't go chasing him. You call me, understand?"

He handed me his card. It read JOSHUA WATERS, ESSEX COUNTY INVESTIGATOR. There was a phone number on the bottom. I thanked him and got out of the car. He pulled out and I waved good-bye. As I trudged up the walk, I thought maybe I smelled garlic but that could have been my imagination.

I used my key to get inside. "Mom?"

There was no reply.

"I'm home," I called out, louder this time. "Mom?"

Still no reply.

I headed into the kitchen. There was nothing on the stove.

There was no smell of garlic. I checked the time. Six P.M. Mom probably wasn't home from therapy yet. That was it. I opened up the refrigerator to grab a drink, but when I did, I saw immediately that there was no new food in it.

Hadn't Mom said she went food shopping?

My breathing got a little funny. I called her cell phone. No answer. I hung up after the fifth ring.

Okay, Mickey, stay calm.

But I couldn't. My hand started shaking. When my phone buzzed, I felt a sense of relief. It had to be Mom. I looked at the caller ID. It was Spoon. I started freaking out. I hit Ignore and dialed the Coddington Rehab Center. I asked for Christine Shippee. When she got on the line, I asked, "Is my mother still there?"

"What are you talking about? Why would your mother be here?"

My heart sank. "She didn't have outpatient therapy today?"

"No." Then: "Oh no. What happened, Mickey? Where is she?"

Here is how stupid I am: I actually went outside and expected to see my mother pull up. So many emotions ricocheted through my brain. I just wanted them to stop. I just wanted to be numb. I longed for that, for feeling absolutely nothing, and then I realized that was what my mom craved too. Look where that led her.

I called Mom's cell phone again. This time, I waited until the voice mail picked up.

"Hi, it's Kitty. Leave me a message at the beep."

I swallowed hard and tried unsuccessfully to keep the pleading from my voice. "Mom? Please call me, okay? Please?"

I didn't cry. But I came close. When I hung up, I wondered what to do. For a little while I just stared at the phone, willing it to ring. But I was done willing and hoping. I had to start getting real.

I thought about how my mom's face had beamed this morning. I thought about how the poison had been out of her system for the past six weeks and how much hope we both had. I didn't want to do this, but I had no choice.

The phone was in my hand. I dialed the number for the first time.

Uncle Myron answered immediately. "Mickey?"

"I can't find Mom."

"Okay," he said. It was almost as though he'd been expecting my call. "I'll handle it."

"What do you mean, you'll handle it? Do you know where she is?"

"I can find out in a few minutes."

I was going to ask how, but there was no time to waste. "I want to go with you," I said.

"I don't think that's a good idea. Let me handle—"

"Myron?" I cut him off. "Please don't play those patronizing games with me. Not now. Not with my mother."

There was a brief silence. Then he said, "I'll pick you up on the way."

chapter 9

THE SATURN RINGS ROUNDABOUT MOTEL was located beneath an overpass on Route 22. The neon sign advertised hourly rates, free Wi-Fi, and color television, as if some rivals might only be using black-and-white ones. The motel was, as the name suggested, round, but that wasn't the first thing you noticed. The first thing you noticed was the filth. The Saturn Rings was the kind of seedy and dirty place that made you want to dunk your whole body in a giant bottle of hand sanitizer.

Myron's Ford Taurus—the one Mom had used to drop me off at school just ten hours earlier, the one she sang along with the radio in and wrote me a tardy excuse—was parked in the motel lot. Myron had put a GPS in his car. I don't know why. Maybe he suspected something like this would happen.

For a moment we just stared at the Taurus in silence. Provocatively dressed women tottered around in too-high heels. They had hollow eyes and sunken cheeks, as if death had already halfway claimed them.

I could hear my breath coming in shallow gasps.

"Any chance I can persuade you to stay in the car?" Myron asked.

I didn't bother answering. We both got out. I wondered how Myron would figure out what room she'd be in, but it didn't take much. We headed into a lobby with barely enough room for the sole vending machine. The man behind the desk wore an undershirt that covered about half his enormous belly. Myron slipped him a hundred-dollar bill. He made it disappear, burped, and said, "Room two-twelve in the C Ring."

We walked to the room in silence. I want to say that I still had hope, but if some was there, I pushed it away. Why? I wondered. Less than a year ago we were a happy, healthy family taking that simple bliss for granted. I pushed that thought away too. Enough with the self-pity.

When we reached her door, Myron and I exchanged a glance. He hesitated, so now I took the lead. I pounded on the door. We waited for someone to open it. No one did. I pounded again. I put my ear against it. Still no answer.

Myron found the floor maid. It cost him twenty dollars this time. She swiped the lock and the door opened. The light was off when we entered. Myron pulled back the curtain. My mom was sprawled out alone on the bed. I wanted so very much to run out of the room or squeeze my eyes shut.

Nothing about a junkie is pretty.

I moved over to the bed and gently shook her shoulder. "Mom?"

"I'm so sorry, Mickey." She started to cry. "I'm so sorry."

"It's going to be okay."

"Please don't hate me."

"Never," I said. "I could never hate you."

We drove her back to rehab. Christine Shippee met us in the lobby, took my mother by the hand, and led her past the security door. I heard Mom's pathetic sniffles cease as the door slammed closed behind her. I glanced at Myron. There may have been pity in his eyes, but what I mostly saw was disgust.

A few minutes later Christine Shippee came back out. Her stroll had her customary no-nonsense bearing. That used to give me confidence. Not anymore.

"Kitty can't have any visitors for at least the next three weeks," she announced.

I didn't like that. "Not even me?"

"No visitors, Mickey." She turned her gaze on me. "Not even you."

"Three weeks?"

"At the very least."

"That's crazy."

"We know what we're doing," Christine Shippee said.

I made a scoffing sound. "Right, sure. I can see that."

Myron said, "Mickey . . ."

But I wasn't done. "I mean, you did such a great job last time."

"It's not uncommon for an addict to have a relapse," she said. "I warned you about this, remember?"

I thought about how my mom had smiled at me, how she told me that she was home preparing spaghetti and meatballs, how she even supplemented her original bogus meal with garlic bread. Lies. All lies.

I stormed out. The sky was a black canvas, not a star in it. I searched for the moon but couldn't find that either. I wanted to scream or hit something. Myron came out a few minutes later and unlocked the car.

"I'm really sorry," Uncle Myron said.

I said nothing. He hated my mother and knew this would happen. He must enjoy being right. We drove a few minutes in silence before Myron broke it.

"We can cancel the trip to Los Angeles, if you want."

I thought about it. There was nothing I could do here. Christine had made it clear that she wouldn't let me see my mother tomorrow. Plus my grandparents were already on their way out there. They wanted to see their son's burial place. I understood that. I wanted to see it again too.

"Don't cancel," I said.

Myron nodded. There was no more conversation. When we got home, I hurried down to the basement, closing the door behind me. I did my homework. Mrs. Friedman had assigned us a term paper on the French Revolution. I started working on it, trying to focus hard so I could get rid of other thoughts. I lift weights four days a week but missed today, so I dropped to the floor and did three sets of sixty push-ups. It felt great. I grabbed a shower. At midnight, I climbed into bed and tried to read a book but the words just swam by in a muddy haze. I flicked off the light and sat in the darkness.

No way I was going to fall asleep.

Myron hadn't hooked up a television down here yet. I considered going up to the den and watching *SportsCenter* or something, but I didn't want to run into my uncle. I picked up my phone and texted Ashley for the umpteenth time. I watched for an answer. None came, of course. I considered telling Mr. Waters about her—but what exactly would I say? I thought about it for a few more minutes. I flipped on my laptop and started doing searches on Ashley's "parents," but that got me very little. Mr. Kent was indeed Dr. Kent, a cardiologist at Valley Hospital. Mrs. Kent was, per Ashley, an attorney working at a big firm in Roseland. So what?

At one A.M., my phone buzzed. I jumped for it, hoping against hope it was Ashley. It wasn't. It was Ema: **u awake?**

I texted back that I was.

Ema: **should we try to break into Bat Lady's again tomorrow?**

Me: **Can't. Going to L.A.**

Ema: **why?**

And then I surprised myself and did something truly out of character. I typed the truth: **Visiting my dad's grave.**

For nearly five minutes there was no answer. I started to scold myself. Who just blurts something like that? Okay, maybe it was a weak moment. It had been a horrendous, confusing, emotional day. I tried to think of what to type, how to backtrack, when another text came in.

Ema: **look in your backyard**

I slid out of bed and made my way to the window in the laundry room—one that faced out back. In the distance, I saw someone—I assumed it was Ema—flashing the light on her cell phone.

Me: **Gimme five.**

It took less. I slipped on a pair of shorts and a T-shirt and headed into the yard. Not surprisingly, Ema was in black, fully "gothed" up in vampire mode. Her earrings had skulls and crossbones on them. The silver stud she normally wore in her eyebrow had been replaced with a silver hoop.

She jammed her hands in her pockets. Her eyes drifted toward the basketball hoop. "Must help," she said.

"What?"

"Basketball," Ema said. "Having a passion like that."

"It does." Then I asked, "Do you have one?"

"A passion?"

"Yes."

Her eyes flicked to the right. "Not really."

"But?"

She shook her head. "This whole thing is weird."

"What is?"

"You being nice to me."

I sighed. "You're not going to start that again."

"I'm the fat outcast. You're the new hot boy being eyed by Rachel Caldwell."

"Rachel Caldwell? You think?"

Ema rolled her eyes. "Men."

I almost smiled and then I remembered. It's funny how you can let yourself forget for seconds, how even in the heat of the horrible you can have moments when you fool yourself into thinking it might all be okay.

"Listen, I'm the real outcast here," I said. "I'm the new boy with the dead dad and junkie mom."

"Your mom's a junkie?"

More blurting. I closed my eyes. When I opened them again, Ema had moved a little closer. She stared into my eyes with the softest look.

"You better not be looking at me with pity," I said.

She ignored my outburst. "Tell me about your mom."

And again—don't ask me why—I did. I'd never had a friend like her, I guess. That would be the easiest explanation. She had known that I was in trouble, and now, at one in the morning, she had made it her business to be here for me. But I think that there was something deeper at work. Ema had that way about her. She just got it. It was as though she already knew the answers and just wanted to make it better.

So I told her. I told her everything. When I finished, Ema shook her head and said, "Garlic bread. Wow."

That was what I meant—about her getting it.

"You must be so angry," Ema said.

I shook my head. "It's not her fault."

"Bull. Do you know what an enabler is?"

I did. An enabler is someone who helps a loved one act in a destructive matter. In a way, she was right. I was making excuses. But how do you make someone understand . . . ?

"If it wasn't for having me," I said slowly, "my mother would have been one of the greatest tennis players in the world. She would have been rich and famous instead of a widowed junkie with nothing."

"Not nothing," Ema said. "She has you."

I waved her away, afraid to speak because I knew that my voice would crack.

Ema didn't push it. Again she somehow knew that would be the wrong move. We sat outside together in silence for a few minutes. It was nearing two in the morning.

"Won't your parents wonder where you are?" I asked.

Her face closed like a steel gate. "No."

And now I knew not to push it. A few minutes later, we

said good-bye. Once again I asked her if I could walk her home. She frowned at me. "I'm serious," I said. "It's late. I don't like you walking alone. Where do you live?"

"Another time," she said.

"Why?"

"Just . . . another time, okay?"

I wasn't sure what else to say here, so I went with, "Okay." Then I added, "But promise me one thing."

Ema looked wary. "What?"

"You'll text me when you get home."

She offered up a small smile and shook her head. "You can't be for real."

"Promise me or I walk you home."

"Fine," she said with a sigh, "I promise, I promise."

Myron's backyard was against the neighbors.' Ema headed out that way. I watched her walk away, her back hunched a little, and I wondered how it was, when I swore I wouldn't connect with anyone, that she already meant so much to me. I watched until she vanished from sight, then I started back to the house. The basketball was lying on the ground outside. I picked it up and spun it on my finger. I looked at the hoop, but no, it was too late. I might wake up the neighbors. I spun the ball again and headed for the back door when something made me stop.

I pushed my back against the wall of the house so I could stay out of sight. My heart started thumping hard in my chest. I put down the ball and slowly slid toward the right, near the garage. I kept low and peered around the corner toward the street in front of Myron's house. And there, parked on the corner maybe two hundred yards away from the house, was a black car with tinted windows.

It looked like the same car I'd seen today at basketball— the same car I'd seen at Bat Lady's house.

I debated my next move. I remembered Mr. Waters telling me to call him if I saw the bald guy again, but come on, it was two in the morning. His cell phone was probably off. And if not, did I really want to wake him and his whole family and—what?—wait for him to maybe drive over? The car would probably be gone by then.

No, this was on me.

I wasn't particularly afraid—or maybe curiosity just won out over fear. Hard to say. When I was ten, my family spent a year in the Amazon rain forest in Brazil. The local chieftain was an expert in hand-to-hand combat, using an offshoot of what was more popularly known as Brazilian jujitsu. I've practiced martial arts ever since, in those obscure corners of the globe, mostly as a way to keep in shape for basketball. To date, I had only used these skills once. They had worked— maybe a little too well.

Whatever, it gave me confidence, even if it might be false confidence. I sprinted behind the Gorets' house next door. My goal was to move from house to house and sneak up on the car from behind. Three houses to go. No reason to stall. I peeked out from behind the Gorets' azaleas and dashed to the Greenhalls. They owned a farm up north and were never home.

A minute later I was hiding behind a bush maybe ten yards away from the black car with the tinted windows. Now that I was this close, I could make out the license plate. A30432. I took out my cell phone and checked the plate number Ema had texted to me. The number was the same.

No doubt now—it was the same black car.

I glanced out from the bush. The car's engine was off. There were no signs of movement or life. The black car could be just parked and empty.

So now what do I do?

Do I just approach and start slamming my palms on the window, demanding answers? That seemed somewhat logical. It also seemed kind of stupid. Do I sit here and wait? For how long? And what if the car drives off? Then what?

I was still hunched behind the bush, trying to decide what to do, when the decision was made for me. The front passenger door opened and the bald guy stepped out. He still wore the dark suit, and despite the hour, he even had the sunglasses on.

For a moment the man stood perfectly still, his back to the bush. Then he slowly turned his head and said, "Mickey."

Gulp.

I had no idea how he had seen me, but it didn't matter now. I stood up. He stared at me from behind those sunglasses, and in spite of the heat, I swear I felt a chill.

"You have questions," the bald man said to me. He spoke with one of those exaggerated British accents that almost sound phony. Like he'd gone to some fancy prep school and wanted to make sure you knew it. "But you're not yet ready for the answers."

"What does that mean?"

"It means," he said, still with that accent, "just what it sounds like."

I frowned. "It sounds like something you'd read on a bad fortune cookie."

There was the hint of a smile on the bald man's face. "Don't tell anyone about us."

"Like who?"

"Like anyone. Like your uncle."

"Myron? What would I tell him anyway? I don't know anything. Who exactly are you? Or, as you put it, us?"

"You'll know," he said, "when the time is right."

"And when will that be?"

The man slid back into the car. He never seemed to hurry, but every moment was almost supernaturally fast and fluid.

"Wait!" I shouted.

I moved quickly, trying to reach the car door before it closed. "What were you doing in that house? Who are you?"

But it was too late. He slammed the door shut. The car started up. Now, as I semi-planned earlier, I slapped the tinted windows with my palm. "Stop!"

The car started to pull out. Without thought I jumped on

the hood. Like you see in the movies. But here is what you don't see in the movies: there is really no place to grab on to. I went for that area near the windshield but my fingers couldn't get a grip. The car moved forward, stopped short, and I went flying.

I managed somehow to land on my feet, stumble, and stay upright. I stood now in front of the car, daring them to run me down. Even the front windshield was tinted, but I stared through it toward the passenger seat, trying to imagine I was eye to eye with the bald man. For a few moments, nothing happened. I stayed in front of the car.

"Who are you?" I asked again. "What do you want with me?"

I heard the passenger window slide down. I was tempted to go to it, but that might be a sucker move. Maybe the man just wanted me to move out of the way so he could drive off.

"Bat Lady said my father is still alive," I shouted.

And, to my surprise, I got a reply. "She shouldn't have said that."

My heart stopped. "Is he?"

There was a long silence.

"Is my father still alive?" I demanded.

I put my hands on the hood, my fingers digging into the metal almost as though I was going to lift the car and shake the answer out of it.

"We'll talk," the man said.

"Don't give me that—"

And then, without warning, the car flew into reverse. I fell forward onto the street, scraping my hands on the pavement. When I looked up, the car spun around and disappeared around the bend.

chapter 10

IT WAS TWO FIFTEEN when I slipped quietly back into the house. My cell phone buzzed. It was a text from Ema: **home. happy?**

Me: **Ecstatic.**

I started tiptoeing toward the basement door when I heard voices coming from upstairs. At first I figured that it was the television, but no, one voice belonged to Myron. The other—hello—was female.

Hmm.

I moved toward the stairs. The light was off in Myron's bedroom, but it was on in the office. The office, as Myron had told me maybe a million times, used to be my dad's bedroom, and before Myron moved to the basement, he and my father had shared it. Myron often regaled me with stories of the lame stuff they used to do together in that room—play board games like Risk and Stratego, trade baseball cards, set up their own Nerf basketball leagues. Sometimes, when no one was in the house, I would go in the room and try to imagine my father as a child in there. But nothing ever came to me. The renovation had stripped the room of any memorabilia. It looked like an accountant's office.

I moved upstairs and stopped by the door. Myron was on the computer, video chatting—at two in the morning? What was up with that?

"I can't come now," I heard Myron say.

A woman's voice said, "I understand. I can't either."

Who was Myron talking to? Wait—was he trying to hook up online? And neither of them wanted to make the trip to the other's town? Oh, gross.

"I know," Myron said.

"Carrie isn't ready," the woman said.

Uh-oh. Who's Carrie? Another woman? Oh, double gross.

"So what do we do?" Myron asked.

The woman said, "I want you to be happy, Myron."

"You make me happy," he said.

"I know. You make me happy too. But maybe we need to be realistic."

They no longer sounded like strangers trying to hook up. They sounded like two people with broken hearts. I peeked into the room again. Myron had his head lowered. I could see a raven-haired woman on the screen.

"Maybe you're right," Myron said. "Maybe we do need to be realistic." He raised his eyes to meet hers on the screen. "But not tonight, okay?"

"Okay." Then the woman said in the most tender voice I'd ever heard, "I love you so much."

"I love you so much too," Myron said.

I didn't know what to do here. I had no idea who this woman was or what they were talking about. I hadn't asked Myron if he had a girlfriend or anything, mostly because I didn't much care.

Whatever, I came up here because I heard voices. I didn't feel good about eavesdropping like this. I took two steps back and quietly padded back down to my bedroom in the basement. I got ready for bed and slipped under the covers.

I wondered about how sad Myron and the woman sounded. I wondered who Carrie was and why Myron couldn't be with her right now. But I didn't wonder about it very long. In the morning, we would fly to Los Angeles and see my father's grave. I figured that thought would keep me up the rest of the night. Instead I dropped off in seconds.

Don't get me wrong—I'm still getting to know them, but as far as I can tell, my grandparents are the coolest grandparents in the history of the world.

Ellen and Al Bolitar—my grandmother likes to joke that they're "El-Al, like the Israeli airline"—greeted us at LAX airport. Grandma sprinted toward Myron and me, arms

116

wide open, hugging us as though we were innocent men just released from serving an unjust prison term, which is to say, like a grandmother should. She hugged us with everything she had and then she looked us over, inspecting us to make sure that everything was how it should be.

"You both look so handsome," Grandma said to me.

I didn't feel handsome. I wore one of Myron's suits. The fit was far from perfect. Grandpa trailed, using a cane and moving too slowly. Myron and I both kissed the old man on the cheek because that was how we all wanted it. Grandpa was still pale and thin from his recent open-heart surgery. I pushed away the feelings of guilt over his condition, but it was hard to escape the fact that I felt at least partially responsible. Grandpa wouldn't have any of that. In fact, he liked to say that I saved his life that day. I had my doubts. As though sensing that, Grandpa gave my shoulder an extra squeeze. I can't tell you why, but that squeeze comforted me like nothing else could.

Myron had a rental car waiting. We drove to the graveyard in silence. Grandma and I sat in the back. She held my hand. She didn't ask about my mother, though she had to know. I loved her for that.

When we reached the graveyard parking lot, I felt my entire body shudder. Myron turned off the car. We all stepped out of the car in the silence. The sun beat down upon us.

"It's up the hill," Myron said. "Maybe I can get you a wheelchair, Dad?"

Grandpa waved him off. "I'll walk to my son's grave."

We made the trek in silence. Grandpa, leaning heavily on his cane, led the way. Grandma and I followed him. Myron brought up the back. As we neared my father's burial spot, Myron caught up to me and asked, "You okay?"

"Fine," I said, picking up my pace.

No headstone marked my father's gravesite yet.

For a long time, no one spoke. The four of us just stood there. Cars from the adjacent highway zoomed by without a care, without the slightest concern that just yards away a devastated family grieved. Without warning Grandpa started reciting the Kaddish, the Hebrew prayer for the dead, from memory. We were not religious people, far from it, so I was a bit surprised. Some things, I guess, we do out of tradition, out of ritual, out of need.

"Yit'gadal v'yit'kadash sh'mei raba . . ."

Myron started to cry. He was like that—overly expressive—the kind of guy who cried at a greeting card commercial. I looked off and tried to keep my face steady. A strange feeling enveloped me. I didn't believe Bat Lady, but today, standing by my beloved father's grave, missing him so much I wanted to rip my own heart out, I was oddly un-moved. Why? Why, I asked myself, am I not totally devas-tated by my father's final resting spot?

And a small voice in my head whispered, *Because he isn't here . . .*

With his hands clasped and his head lowered, Grandpa

finished the long prayer with the words "Aleinu v'al kol Yis'ra'eil v'im'ru. Amen."

Myron and Grandma joined in for that fourth and final amen, making the word sound more like "oh-main." I stayed silent. For several minutes, no one moved. We were all lost in our own thoughts.

I flashed back to the first time I had been in this cemetery, at my father's funeral, just me and my mom. Mom had been stoned to the point of oblivion. She made me promise that we wouldn't tell anybody about Dad's death because Uncle Myron would claim that she was an unfit parent and seek custody. I looked down at the small placard that was there until a gravestone would be ready. The placard had been there on that day too. BRAD BOLITAR, it read, in plain black ink on a white index card in a weather-protected plastic case.

After another silent minute had passed, Grandpa shook his head and said, "This should never be." He stopped and looked up at the sky. "A father should never have to say the Kaddish for his son."

With that, he started back down the path. Myron and Grandma followed. They looked back at me. I took a step closer to the loose dirt. My father, the man I had loved like no other, lay six feet below me.

I didn't feel it, but that didn't mean it wasn't so. I stared down now at the placard and didn't move.

Behind me I heard Myron say, "Mickey?"

I didn't reply or react because, well, I couldn't. I was still staring at the placard, feeling my already teetering world spin me off my feet again. I saw Dad's name. I saw the plain black ink on the white index card. But now I saw something else too. A drawing. The drawing was small and in the corner of the index card, but there was no mistaking what it was. An emblem of a colorful butterfly with what might have been animal eyes on the wings. I had seen it before—at Bat Lady's house.

It was the same emblem as on those T-shirts in that old picture.

We said good-bye at the airport. Hugs and kisses were exchanged. Grandma said to both Myron and me, "You'll come down for Thanksgiving."

Grandma didn't ask—she told, and I loved her for that. I regret that my grandparents hadn't been a bigger part of my life until now, but Mom and Dad had their reasons, I guess.

My grandparents caught a plane back to Florida; Myron and I grabbed one half an hour later to Newark. The flight was full. Myron volunteered to take the middle seat. I had the window. We shoehorned ourselves into our seats. Coach seats are not designed for people our height. Two little old ladies sat in front of us. Their feet could barely touch the ground, but that didn't stop them from reclining the seat with great strength into our knees. I spent the four hours with an old lady's scalp in my face.

At one point during the flight, I almost asked Myron about what I'd seen at two A.M. I almost asked him who the raven-haired woman was and who Carrie was, but I didn't because I knew that would lead to a longer conversation and I wasn't really in the mood to open up.

After landing, we grabbed Myron's car from long-term parking and started up the Garden State Parkway. Neither of us spoke for the first twenty minutes of the drive. When we passed our exit, I finally said something.

"Where are we going?"

"You'll see," Myron said.

Ten minutes later, we pulled into the strip mall lot. Myron put the car in park and smiled at me. I looked out the windshield, then back at Myron.

"You're taking me for ice cream?"

"Come on," Myron said.

"You're kidding me, right?"

When we entered the SnowCap ice cream parlor, a woman in a wheelchair greeted us. She was probably in her early twenties and had this big, wonderful smile. "Hey, you're back," she said to Myron. "What can I get you?"

"Set up my nephew here with your SnowCap Melter. I need to talk to your father for a minute."

"Sure thing. He's in the back room."

Myron left us. The woman in the wheelchair held out her hand. "I'm Kimberly."

I shook it. "I'm Mickey."

"Sit over there," Kimberly said, gesturing to a chair. "I'll whip you up a SnowCap Melter."

The Melter was the approximate size and dimensions of a Volkswagen Bug. Kimberly wheeled it over with that big, lovely smile. I wondered why she was in the chair, but of course I'd never ask.

I looked at the huge plate of ice cream and toppings and whipped cream. "We're supposed to eat this alone?"

She laughed. "We'll do what we can."

We dug in. I don't want to exaggerate, but the SnowCap Melter was the greatest thing anyone has ever eaten in the history of the world. I started eating it so fast I feared getting one of those ice cream headaches. Kimberly was having fun watching me.

"What does Myron want with your father?" I asked her.

"I think that your uncle has realized a universal truth."

"What's that?"

Kimberly's smile fled, and I swear I felt a cold breeze against my neck. "You do what you have to do to protect the young."

"I'm not following."

"You will."

"What does that mean?"

Kimberly blinked, looked away. "Sixteen years ago, my older sister was murdered. She was only sixteen years old."

I had no idea what to say to that. Finally I asked, "What does Myron have to do with that?"

"Not just Myron," she said. "Your mother had something to do with it. So did your father."

I put down the spoon. "I don't understand any of this. Are you saying my parents hurt—"

"No!" She cut me off. "Your parents would never hurt anyone. Never."

"How do you know my parents?"

"I don't. But understand something now, Mickey. None of this is a coincidence."

My head was spinning.

"Don't tell Myron we talked, okay?"

I nodded.

"Eat the ice cream," she whispered.

I took another bite. The door to the back room opened. Myron appeared. Kimberly leaned over to me and whispered into my ear, "Laugh like you just heard the funniest joke in the world."

I was going to ask her why, but for some reason I trusted and liked her. So I did as she asked. It felt a little forced, but then she laughed with me. Her laugh had a contagious quality. It made it easier for me to let go. Kimberly leaned again and whispered, "One more time. We don't want your uncle to ask what we're talking about."

So I laughed again—and again she joined me. Myron stared at me with puppy-dog eyes and a small, sad smile. Kimberly wheeled herself away. Confused, lost, I let my laugh fade away. I didn't know what to do when my phone vibrated. I checked the caller ID and saw it was Spoon. I put the phone to my ear.

"What's up?" I asked him.

"Mickey?" I could hear the excitement in his voice. Spoon was, in fact, so excited that he skipped his customary non sequitur. "I got something."

"Got what?"

"Ashley's locker."

"What about it?"

"I know who broke into it."

chapter 11

EMA, SPOON, AND I met up in the parking lot the next morning before school. We sat on the curb. Ema had her laptop. Spoon wore sunglasses today. He had a briefcase, a real, live briefcase like you might see a businessman in a movie use. I can't remember ever seeing one in person before. Spoon played with the combination lock and flicked it open. I looked inside. There was nothing but a flash drive. Spoon arched his eyebrow above the sunglasses as he pulled it out and locked up the case.

"What you are about to see," Spoon said with maximum drama, whipping off his sunglasses, "must forever remain with us."

He handed Ema the flash drive. Ema sighed. "What is this?"

"The surveillance video," Spoon said. "You see, the school

has a pretty extensive security system—eighteen security cameras covering most entrances and corridors. I realized that no one would have broken that lock during the day. Someone would have noticed. I also realized that someone must have broken it recently because a broken lock, dangling like that, would have been reported within a few days. So I used my key to get into the security office. They store everything digitally. I found Camera Fourteen—that's the one that covers Ashley's locker—and started reviewing the night before we saw her broken lock."

"How long did that take you?" I asked.

Spoon grinned. "Almost no time at all. You see, the cameras are motion sensitive, so most nights they just stay off."

Ema plugged the flash drive into her computer port. We all huddled around the screen when two hands reached in and snagged the laptop away.

"Hey!" Ema said.

"Well, well, well," a now-familiar, grating voice said. "What do we have here?"

I turned around and saw Troy holding the laptop. Buck was next to him. Behind them were assorted jock-toughs. I think there were five of them, maybe six. It was hard to tell. The varsity jackets tended to blend into one big mass.

Spoon said, "What do you guys want?"

"Well, *Arthur*," Buck said, "we just think you're kinda cool and wanted to hang with you?"

Spoon beamed. "Really?"

"Give me back my laptop," Ema said.

They ignored her. I debated how to play this.

"Yeah, sure, we wanna hang with you," Troy said to Spoon. "You got all the right moves. Or movements anyway."

Spoon pushed up his glasses. "Huh?"

"A movement," Troy said. "Like in a bowel movement. Because you smell like one."

Troy raised his hand for a high five. Buck slapped it. The assorted jock-toughs snorted laughter. Spoon looked as though someone had slapped him.

I rose. "Good one. Now give us back the laptop."

Troy smirked and moved a step closer to me. "Make me."

"He will!" Spoon shouted, small tears in his eyes. "Next time he goes to the bathroom!"

I looked back at Spoon and frowned as if to say, *Come on, we're better than that.*

Troy pointed at him. "You want me to kick your ass, Arthur?"

"My name is Spoon!"

"What?"

"That's my nickname," Spoon said. "Spoon." He pointed at Ema. "Like her nickname is Ema." Then he pointed at Buck. "And like his nickname is Wee Wee Pants."

"What the—?" Buck's face went red again. "I'm going to so kick your ass."

I stayed between them and Spoon. "Why don't you deal with me?" I said.

127

Buck's head spun toward me. "You wanna die too?"

"No," I said. "Right now I want the laptop back."

"You want it," Troy said, leaning close enough for me to smell his morning scrambled eggs, holding the laptop in his right hand and wiggling it, "take it from me."

So I did.

When I was in the Amazon studying martial arts, we worked a lot on taking away hand weapons. Naturally I received many lectures on never doing it—in how running away was always far smarter than trying to disarm—but if cornered or forced, I was taught what to do. The key element is surprise. If someone knows you're going for the weapon, sorry, despite what you see in kung fu movies, it is nearly impossible to get the weapon without getting hurt.

Here, of course, there was no weapon danger. So I went for it. When Troy wasn't prepared, I simply snatched the laptop from his rather weak grip. There was also something else working in my favor here: my genetics. I don't take credit for this. It was an accident of birth. My father was a good natural athlete, though he never liked the competitive aspects of sports. My uncle was a pro-caliber basketball player. My mother was a pro-caliber tennis player. So I get it from both sides of the gene pool. I was born with good hand-eye coordination and quickness. Much as you might work on that and parents might try to push it, you can't really teach that stuff.

For a moment, Troy and Buck didn't move. I quickly

handed the laptop back to Ema, never taking my eyes off my adversary—another lesson drummed into me. I turned and prepared for whatever they might do. I knew it had to be something. Troy was the cool senior. I, a lowly sophomore, had shown him up.

Man, it was going to be a long basketball season.

He was about to reach out for me when Ema said, "Troy?"

"What?"

"I know the real reason you're always bothering us." Ema batted her dark eyelashes at him. "Do you maybe, I don't know, have a little crush on me?"

"What? You crazy?"

"Stealing my laptop like that—such a flirt move." Ema batted her eyes at him some more and feigned coquettish. "Rachel Caldwell isn't into you, but who knows? Maybe I'll be. True, I'll have to lose my sense of vision, not to mention smell, to find you attractive, but . . ."

Troy grabbed me by the lapels. I went with it, making my body a little slack as though scared. "You better stay out of my way, Bolitar. You hear me?"

"Hey," I said, putting my hands up in mock surrender. "I'm not the one who came over here to hit on your friend."

That was enough for Troy. Keeping one hand gripping my shirt, he cocked his fist way back, almost like a windup. It was a classic move and when he bullied guys like Spoon, it probably worked. But it was dumb. The shortest distance between two points is a straight line. You snap for the weak zones—nose, throat, groin, eyes. You don't take your time and pull your fist back.

There were several moves I could make here, but I decided to go with the one that would leave the least damage. I quickly trapped the hand on my chest with my forearm, grabbing on to the fingers. I jerked to the right, knocking him slightly off balance. The final part of the move—actually this all took less than a second—was to sweep the leg.

Troy went down on the pavement.

I didn't know what would happen next, if he'd be dumb enough to try to stand or dive for my legs, but I was ready.

"What's going on here?"

It was Ms. Owens. I let go of Troy. He jumped up with as much dignity as he could muster, trying to give off an I-was-just-about-to-beat-your-butt attitude. I didn't challenge it.

"I said, what's going on here?"

There were loads of nothings muttered. Troy and Buck and the assorted jock-toughs seemed to fade away. Ms. Owens glared at me for a moment and then she left too.

Ema stood next to me. "Getting in a fight with a popular senior. Pissing off a schoolteacher and the local chief of police. Hanging with two major-league losers." She slapped my back. "Welcome to high school."

We still had time before the bell rang.

The three of us were back huddled around Ema's laptop.

She clicked the video icon. The B corridor at school appeared on the screen. I expected the feed to be grainy or black-and-white, but it looked high-def. Ema hit the Play button, and a man came into view. He wasn't a teacher. He wasn't a student. He wasn't staff.

He looked like a pure hoodlum.

He wore a sleeveless T-shirt, low-slung jeans, and bad facial stubble. Thick gold chains hung from his neck. In his right hand, he carried a crowbar.

There was also a tattoo on this face.

I looked over at Spoon. "Tattoo on the face. Isn't that what Mrs. Kent said the man who broke into their house had?"

Spoon nodded. "It has to be the same guy."

What could this hoodlum have to do with Ashley?

The video didn't come with sound, but the silence was kind of deafening. Tattoo Face stopped walking in front of the locker. Using the crowbar, he smashed Ashley's lock. He opened the locker and stepped back. Tattoo Face looked inside and then, even without sound, you could tell he was angry and probably cursing.

The locker was empty.

A moment or two later, Tattoo Face stormed away. "That's it," Spoon said.

Ema stopped the tape.

"So now what?" I asked. "Do we show this to the cops?"

Spoon pushed the glasses up his nose. "You're kidding, right?"

131

"This guy probably broke into the Kent household. We have video of his face."

"Video I stole from the security room at school," Spoon said. "How would we explain that? I don't trust cops." Spoon turned to Ema and puffed out his chest. "See, I have a police record. Is it true that chicks like dangerous men?"

"*Men* maybe," Ema said. "But he's right, Mickey. You can't go to the cops. Spoon here will get in trouble, for one, but also, hey, remember who's police chief in this town."

Troy's father, Chief Taylor. Oh boy, did I remember. Not only did I have a problem with the Taylor clan, but clearly Uncle Myron didn't get along with them either.

"Okay, so we don't go to the cops," I said. "So what do we do next?"

Ema clicked on the screen again. The video feed came up. She clicked an arrow and the feed started going backward in slow motion. She stopped it and then zoomed in so that we had a pretty clear look at the side of Tattoo Face's cheek— the one with the tattoo.

"I have a thought," Ema said, "but it's probably a long shot."

Spoon and I signaled that we were anxious to hear it.

"I know a guy. A tattoo artist named Agent. He did my stuff."

"Okay," I said.

"Anyway, the tattoo community is a pretty tight one. Everyone knows everyone. These guys are artists, and this looks like pretty special work. So what I'm thinking is, we show this photograph to Agent. Maybe he can tell us who the artist is."

I looked at Spoon. He nodded that he liked the idea. "Okay," I said. "Let's do it."

"One problem," Ema said. "There really is no public transportation to get there, and it's too far to walk. We need to get someone to drive us."

"Don't worry about it," I said.

Ema frowned. "What does that mean?"

"I can drive us."

"You're not sixteen yet."

"Don't worry about that either," I said. And then the bell rang.

Mrs. Friedman had a surprise for us in history class.

"We are going to do a project on the French Revolution," she said. "Everyone will need a partner, so please choose one."

I didn't know anyone in the class, so I figured I would wait until the end and take whoever was left. Everyone else in the class moved in a flurry, joining up with friends, afraid to be left out. Everyone, that is, except Rachel Caldwell. She stared at me and smiled. Even though I was sitting, I felt my knees go a little weak. People tapped Rachel on the shoulder, called her name, tried to get her attention. She ignored them and continued to meet my gaze.

"Well?" she asked me.

"Well what?" I said.

I just keep stunning her with the great one-liners.

"Do you want to be history partners?" she asked.

"Sure," I said.

Mrs. Friedman clapped to get everyone's attention. "Okay, people, if you have your partner, move your chair next to theirs so I can tell you the assignment."

I rose and grabbed my chair. I stopped for a moment, feeling shy, but Rachel slid over and signaled for me to move next to her. I did. She smelled like, well, a beautiful girl. I started to feel warm. Rachel Caldwell gave Mrs. Friedman her undivided attention. She took lots of notes. Her notebook was pristine. I tried to pay attention—Mrs. Friedman was indeed giving us an assignment—but the words swam by in a murky haze.

When the bell rang, Rachel turned to me. "When do you want to meet up?"

"Soon," I said.

"How about after school today?"

I remembered that we were going to visit Agent, the tattoo artist. "I can't after school. Maybe tonight?"

"Sounds like a plan. Why don't you call me?"

"Okay, sure."

Rachel waited. I didn't know what for. Then she said, "You don't know my number."

"Oh. Right."

"You're probably going to need it," she said. "I mean, it's going to be hard to call me without the phone number."

I nodded sagely. "You make a good point," I said.

She laughed. "Give me your phone."

I did as she asked, handing over my cell phone. She started typing. "Here's my number."

"Thank you."

"Talk to you later." She handed me back the phone and started to leave.

"Bye."

Five minutes later, I was at the lunch table with Ema. Ema studied my face and said, "What's with the stupid grin?"

"What stupid grin?"

She frowned. "I called Agent. He can meet us after school."

"Good." Then I said, "You're not even fifteen yet, are you?"

"So?"

"So how did you get tattoos? I thought you had to be eighteen."

"You can be younger if you get your parents' permission."

"So that's what you did?"

"Don't worry about it," Ema said with a little edge in her voice. "How are you going to drive us there without a license?"

"Don't worry about it," I said, mimicking her tone.

Ema took a bite of her submarine sandwich. She finished

chewing and tried to sound nonchalant. "How was your trip to Los Angeles?"

"Fine. But after you left the other day, I saw our friend from Bat Lady's house."

I told her about it. Ema was so good at zeroing in on me when I spoke, making it easier to talk, making the rest of the world sort of fade away. She didn't just show you that she cared—you felt it.

When I finished, Ema said, "We have to go back to Bat Lady's house."

"I don't know."

"And they told you not to tell anyone, right?"

"Right."

"Yet you told me."

"Yeah, I guess I did. But wait, they said don't tell anyone about us. You already knew about them."

She smiled. "I like the way you find loopholes."

Spoon came over and slammed his tray down next to us. "Every day in the United States, two hundred new jail cells are constructed. I don't want one of them to have my name on it."

"I told you," I said. "We won't go to the cops."

He sat down and started eating. Two minutes later, I heard Spoon mutter, "Oh. My. God." His eyes widened as if he were witnessing the dead being brought to life. I spun toward where he was gazing and saw Rachel Caldwell heading toward us. She was carrying a plate of cookies.

"Hi, guys," Rachel said with a smile that didn't just dazzle. It picked you up and shook you hard and then just dropped you back in your seat.

Ema frowned and crossed her arms. Spoon said, "Will you marry me?"

Rachel laughed. "You're so adorable."

A swoon. A Spoon swoon, if you will.

"I don't want to bother you guys," Rachel said, "but we were just having a cheerleader bake sale. Lame, right?"

"Very," Ema said, arms still crossed. I shot her a look.

"Anyway, my cookies are pretty awful, so no one bought them, so I figured before I threw them out . . ."

"Thank you," I said.

She quickly put them down on the table and shyly walked away.

"The future ex–Mrs. Spoon," Spoon said. Then, thinking about it, "Or would she be Fork? I must work on that."

"You do that," I said. I picked up a chocolate chip cookie and took a bite. "Not bad," I said.

Ema rolled her eyes into the back of her head. "Of course you like her cookies. They could be made from baby powder and wood shavings and you'd still like them."

"No, seriously, try one."

"Pass," Ema said.

"You know," I said, chewing the rather dry cookie and wondering what to wash it down with, "disliking someone— anyone, really—based on his or her looks is shallow."

Ema rolled her eyes even farther back in her head. "Yeah," she said, "I feel so bad about that. Rachel must be crushed."

"I think she's nice," Spoon said.

"I'm shocked," Ema said. Then looking back at me, "Do you know she used to date your buddy Troy?"

I made a face. "Eew." Then: "Used to, right?"

More eye rolling. "Talk about shallow. The hot cheerleader going for the basketball captain? Only one thing you can conclude from that."

"She's right," Spoon said, looking at me solemnly. He put his hand on my shoulder. "You got to figure a way to become basketball captain."

chapter 12

AFTER SCHOOL, Spoon, Ema, and I walked to Myron's house. I grabbed the car keys from the kitchen, and we got into the Ford Taurus. I flashed back to my father teaching me how to drive. We were in an old stick shift in South Africa. I kept flooding the engine and Dad kept laughing. "Ease up on the clutch," he told me, but I had no idea what that meant. I had just turned fourteen. When we traveled in certain remote parts of the world, we would use other names and identifications. The one in my pocket right now was Robert Johnson. It was best, Dad had said, to use fairly common names when going with a fake ID, something people wouldn't really remember or, if they checked, they'd be overwhelmed with information. Robert Johnson was twenty-one years old, a solid six years older than me. I didn't look twenty-one but when you're my height, you can often pass.

The IDs were also impeccable. I don't know how. I asked my father why we needed them, but he was always a little vague about it. "The work we do," Dad said. "We make enemies."

"Aren't we helping people?" I asked.

"We are."

"So how do you make enemies?"

"If you rescue someone, you're often rescuing them *from* someone." Dad looked off, bit down on his lower lip. "If you're doing good, it's often because someone else is doing evil. Follow me?"

"Yes."

"And those that are doing evil," Dad continued, "aren't afraid to hurt anyone who interferes with their plans."

Ironic, I guess. He was a humanitarian, my father. He survived going against the wishes of despots and dictators in some of the most dangerous and war-torn jungles in the world. He finally settled back in the relative safety of the United States and dies in a car crash driving me to a basketball game.

It was hard not to be angry.

I thought again about Bat Lady telling me my dad might still be alive. Maybe that was what this was all about—finding Ashley, the bald guy in the dark car, Bat Lady herself.

Maybe I was doing all this because of the one chance, the one in a zillion, that she meant it. That it was true.

"Make a right," Ema said. "It's on Route Forty-Six."

As we approached, Spoon started sniggering.

"What?" Ema asked him.

"The name of the tattoo parlor," he said.

"What about it?"

"Tattoos While U Wait," Spoon said. "What kind of name is that? While U Wait? Like, how else would you do it? Rip off your arm and say, 'Here, put a snake on the shoulder, I'll pick it up in the morning'? Of course you wait." He sniggered some more.

Ema looked at me. "We have to leave him in the car."

I nodded. Spoon agreed to be our "lookout."

My first thought when entering Tattoos While U Wait was a surprising one: cleanliness. I expected something gritty and grimy, but this place looked more sterile than a doctor's office. It gleamed. The actual workers and patrons appeared rough around the edges, dressed in jeans and T-shirts and, well, loaded up with piercings and tattoos. Tattoos While U Wait could have been a banquet hall holding the Ema family reunion.

"Hey, Ema," the woman at the front desk—classic biker chick—said. She and Ema pounded fists. I was surprised that they would know her as Ema here. I assume that she told them her nickname. More irony. Ema clearly liked a nickname given to her by that ass-tard Troy Taylor.

We found Agent in the back. There were posters of various Hindu gods on the wall, many in states of meditation. Incense burned, tickling my nose. There was soft music playing, a woman repeating the "So hum" over and over in what I guessed was some kind of mantra.

Agent had just finished a huge back tattoo, an eagle with a shoulder-to-shoulder wingspan. His client was using two mirrors to look at it, like a guy checking the neckline at a hair salon.

"Beautiful work, Agent," the man said.

Agent put his hands together in prayer position. "Don't get it wet for two weeks. Make sure you keep the cream on it. You've done this before."

"I have, yeah."

"Wonderful." When Agent spotted us, his face broke into a smile. "Ema!"

They embraced. "Agent, meet my friend Mickey."

Agent shook my hand. His grip was strong, his hand callused. He had long red hair pulled back, and his long beard had a ponytail holder in it. Naturally he was overloaded with tattoos and piercings. "So nice to meet you, Mickey," he said a little too earnestly.

"Same here."

He looked back at Ema. "Do you have a picture of the tattoo?"

Ema nodded. With the quality of the video feed, Ema was able to get a good, clear close-up of the tattoo. She handed the still shot to Agent. He looked at it for maybe two seconds and said, "Eduardo."

"What?"

"That is definitely Eduardo's work. He has a shop in Newark. Would you like me to call him and see who commissioned this?"

"He'll tell you?" I asked.

Agent smiled at me. "If I request the information, yes, Eduardo will tell me. We aren't attorneys, Mickey. There is no tattoo artist–client confidentiality. There is merely trust. There is a reason you are here, Mickey. There is a flow to the universe, a path it has to inevitably follow."

Oookay, I thought.

"Ema came into this shop for a reason. She ended up asking me to be her tattoo artist. That has led to you being here. Do you understand?"

No, I thought, while saying, "Sure."

"Plus, well, Ema has a pure spirit. A delightful chakra. If Ema tells me you need to find this man, you need to find the man. It is that simple."

Ema blushed. "Thanks, Agent."

He winked at her. I again wondered how they knew each other and how, at her age, she could have so many tattoos, but hey, I had my secrets too.

"Please wait here," Agent said, "whilst I call Eduardo."

Oookay, I thought again. The woman kept singing "So hum." Man, that was getting annoying. I looked out the window. Spoon sat in the car. Ema said, "Maybe we should have left the window open a crack. Like with a dog."

I smiled. A man in front of us was getting a wrist tattoo, the needle scraping the skin. He had his eyes squeezed shut, but tears still leaked out. I thought again about Ashley with her pearls and sweaters and wondered how I had gone from searching for that preppy beauty to a New Age tattoo artist named Agent.

More irony?

"Here you are," Agent said, appearing with a flourish. He handed Ema a slip of paper. The name on it was Antoine LeMaire. The address was in Newark.

"Thank you, Agent," Ema said.

"Yeah," I said. "Thank you."

"I would join you on this quest," Agent said, "but I have another engagement."

Ema said, "Work?"

Agent shook his head. "Yoga class."

"Are you still working with Swami Paul?" Ema asked.

"No. The heat of that Bikram was messing with my red chakra. It was making me angry all the time. I'm all about Kundalini right now. You should try it, both of you. I mean, look at me." He spread his arms. "I'm all white lately."

Oookay.

We started for the door when Agent called out, "Mickey?"

I turned.

"You, like Ema, have a pure spirit. You have blessed energy centers and true balance. You are a protector. You look out for others. You are their shelter."

"Uh, thanks."

"And because of that, you have a certain wisdom. You understand that you know nothing about this man you seek. You should be careful before bringing others into his space."

Agent met my eye and I caught his meaning. I nodded. "Thanks for the heads-up."

He gave me a little bow. "You should consider a tattoo. It would look good."

"I don't think they're for me," I said.

"Yes," Agent said with the most knowing smile on his face. "You are probably right."

chapter 13

WHEN WE GOT BACK IN THE CAR, Ema said, "Put the address in the GPS."

"No," I said.

"What?"

I had caught Agent's warning, but I wasn't sure I needed it. Here was what I knew about Antoine LeMaire: He had broken into a school and Ashley's locker. He had broken in and assaulted Dr. Kent. In short, there was an excellent chance that he was a dangerous man. I could take risks— that was on me—but I wasn't about to drag Spoon and Ema into that particular hazardous zone.

That would be, uh, red chakra.

"It's getting late," I said. "I'll drop you guys off."

"You're kidding," Ema said.

"No. We aren't going when it's dark."

Spoon said, "Maybe we should stop at that lamp store first."

"Huh?"

"So we can buy Mickey a night-light," Spoon continued. "You know, him being scared of the dark and all."

Ema smiled. "Yeah, little Mickey need a nighty-lighty? Maybe a blankee too?"

I just looked at her. She shrugged an apology and said, "Drop off Spoon first."

I did. Spoon directed me to a two-family house on the outskirts of Kasselton. There was a small truck parked in the driveway. The truck had a crossed mop-heads logo on the side. Cute.

When we pulled up, the front door opened. A man and a woman in their forties appeared. The man wore a janitor's uniform. The woman had a business suit. The man was white. The woman was black.

Spoon shouted, "Mom! Dad!"

He ran up the stoop and they all greeted one another as if a hostage standoff had just ended. Ema and I watched in silence. I felt a pang of envy, but I felt a bigger pang of responsibility. Look at this kid with his loving parents. I couldn't risk putting him or Ema in danger.

Spoon pointed at our car. His parents smiled and waved to us. Ema and I waved back. Ema said, "Wow, look at them."

"I know," I said.

They disappeared into the house.

"So what's the plan?" Ema asked.

"We both go home. We do a little online research, see what we can find out about our tattooed friend Antoine LeMaire. We meet up in the morning and discuss."

"Sounds good." She pulled the door handle. "I'll see you tomorrow."

"Wait, I can drop you off."

"No need," Ema said.

"You live around here?"

"Close enough. Bye."

"Wait."

She didn't. She got out of the car and started down the road. I debated following her, but she quickly veered right and vanished into the woods. I thought about pressing the issue, getting out of the car and running after her, but I had my secrets—wasn't Ema entitled to hers too?

I was worried that Uncle Myron might be home. How would I explain driving the car? He knew that I had a fake ID. When he first found Mom and me in that trailer park, I was working under the name Robert Johnson at a nearby Staples. Still, I don't think that he would like me driving illegally to a tattoo parlor or anyplace else, for that matter.

I parked in the garage, grabbed something to eat, and headed down to the basement. I Googled Antoine LeMaire, but nothing useful came up—not even a Facebook page or

Twitter account. Pretty much nothing. I put the address into MapQuest. From the satellite photograph, the area looked pretty seedy. I could also see that it was right next door to a place called the Plan B Go-Go Lounge. I frowned and again thought about where my search for Ashley was taking me.

I looked to the wall of old basketball greats.

"What's all this have to do with Ashley?" I asked out loud.

The posters did not reply.

I heard noise above me and then I heard Myron yell, "Mickey?"

"Homework!" I shouted back. *Homework* was a great word to ward off unwanted guardians. When you yelled, "Homework," parents always left you alone. It worked better than a cross keeping away a vampire.

I stared down at my desk. My laptop was beat up from travel. My dad bought it three years ago when we were in Peru, and so it had been around the world several times over. Funny. I don't have any of his possessions. He had taught me that they were irrelevant. A ring isn't my dad. A watch isn't my dad. None of those things would bring comfort. As my dad had explained to me, no true joy was ever found in a "thing."

But oddly enough, this laptop seemed more personal, more "him," than any of those more classic items might. He had spent time on this laptop. He had composed letters, worked on progress reports, looked up information on this machine. I thought about that sometimes, about his hands on this keyboard.

We each had our own folder—Dad, Mom, and me—and I clicked on his. I moved the files in order from when they were most recently opened. For a moment I was surprised to see one opened only six weeks ago, but then I remembered. Uncle Myron had searched this computer, looking for clues about his brother's fate.

The last file he'd opened—the most recent—was called "Resignation Letter." I clicked on it and the document appeared:

To: The Abeona Shelter

Dear Juan:

It is with a heavy heart, my old friend, that I resign my position with our wonderful organization. Kitty and I will always be loyal supporters. We believe in this cause so much and have given so much to it. In truth, though, we have been more enriched than the young people we've helped. You understand this. We will always be grateful.

It is time, however, for the wandering Bolitars to settle down. I've secured a position back in Los Angeles. Kitty and I like being nomads, but it has been a long time since we stopped long enough to grow roots. Our son, Mickey, needs that, I think. He never asked for this life. He has spent his life traveling, making and then losing friends, and never calling one place home. He needs normalcy now and a chance to pursue his passions, especially basketball. So after much debate, Kitty and I have decided to get him settled into one place for his last three years of high school, and then he can apply to college.

After that, who knows? I never imagined this life for myself. My father used to quote a Yiddish proverb: Man plans, God laughs. Kitty and I hope to return one day. I know that no one really ever leaves the Abeona Shelter. I know I am asking a big thing here. But I hope you'll understand. In the meantime, we will do all we can to make this transition a smooth one.

Yours in Brotherhood,

Brad

I read the letter twice more, my eyes blurring with tears. There was noise coming from upstairs, but I ignored it. I already knew most of what was in this letter, I guess. There were no real surprises. But to see it written out like that, stated so plainly by my now-deceased father, it was like a hand squeezing my heart.

Yes, I had grown weary of the constant travel. I had wanted a normal life, in one community, a place where I could join a school basketball team for an entire season, test my skills with real teammates, make lasting friends, stay in one school, maybe apply to college.

Well congratulations, Mickey. You got what you wanted.

I thought about our lives when my father wrote that letter. We had been so great, hadn't we? Mom and Dad had been happy and in love. Now, thanks to my wants, Dad was dead and the only thing Mom was in love with came out of a needle. And the truth—the unmistakable truth when you looked at it with honest eyes—was that it was my fault.

Nice work, Mickey.

The basement door opened behind me. Myron called down, "Mickey?"

I wiped my eyes. "Homework!"

Myron's voice had a happy-little-singsong quality to it. "You have a visitor."

"What?"

I could hear his footsteps coming down.

More singsong. "There's a young lady here to see you."

I spun around. Myron reached the bottom of the steps with the biggest, goofiest, dorkiest smile I had ever seen on a human being. Behind him, coming into view just now, was Rachel Caldwell.

"Hi," she said.

"Hi," I said. Mr. Romance.

Myron smiled at us like a game-show host. "Do you kids want me to make you popcorn?"

"No, thanks," I said quickly.

"How about you, little lady?"

Little lady? I wanted to die.

"I'm fine, Mr. Bolitar, thank you."

"You can call me Myron."

He was still standing there, smiling like the most pleased jackass. I stared at him, flaring my eyes a little so that he'd catch the hint. He did. Awkwardly. "Oh, right," Myron said. "I'll just leave you two alone then. I'm going to head back upstairs, I guess."

Myron pointed up the stairs with his thumb. Like maybe we didn't know where "upstairs" was.

"Great," I said, hoping to move him along.

Uncle Dork took one step and turned back toward us. "Uh, um, if it's okay—and even if it's not—I'm going to leave the basement door open. It's not that I don't trust you two, but I think Rachel's parents wouldn't approve—"

"Fine!" I said, interrupting him. "Leave the door open."

"Not that I feel like I have to check up on you or anything. I'm sure you're both very responsible teenagers."

I wondered if I would ever in my life feel more mortified. "Thanks, Myron. Bye."

"If you change your mind about the popcorn—"

"You'll be the first to know," I said. "Bye."

Myron finally headed up the stairs. I turned to Rachel, who was smothering a chuckle.

"I'm sorry about my dorky uncle."

"I think he's nice," Rachel said. "By the way, is everyone in your family over seven feet tall? Remind me not to wear flats when I visit you."

I laughed at that, maybe a little too hard, but I needed a laugh.

"I've got two tests next week," Rachel said, "so I thought maybe we could get a jump on the French Revolution project?"

"Sure," I said.

Rachel took in the basement. Myron's posters. Myron's lava lamp (yes, he had one). Myron's beanbag chairs. "Cool room."

"It's my uncle's."

"For real?"

"Yeah. I'm just here temporarily."

"From where?"

"All over," I said.

"Nice vague answer," Rachel said.

"I was trying to be a man of mystery."

"Try harder."

I liked the way she said that.

"So, man of mystery, what were you doing by your girlfriend's locker yesterday?"

I almost said, *She's not really my girlfriend,* but I didn't. "Just checking on something," I said.

"Checking on what?"

"Do you know Ashley?" I asked.

"Not really, no."

I didn't know how much to say here. Rachel looked at me with deep-blue eyes a boy could fall into and never find his way out. And he'd be happy that way. "She left school," I said. "I mean, I haven't seen or heard from her in a week. I don't know where she went."

"And you thought her locker . . . ?"

"I don't know. I thought it might hold a clue or something."

Rachel seemed to consider this. "Ashley is new to the school too, right?"

"Right," I said.

"So maybe she just moved away."

"Maybe," I said.

From upstairs Myron yelled, "How's it going down there? Anybody want some popcorn and apple juice?"

Apple juice?

Rachel smiled at me. I felt my face flush.

Myron shouted down again, "Mickey?"

"Homework!"

chapter 14

LATE THAT NIGHT, while I was getting ready for bed, I got a text. Ema: **can you get out?**

Me: **Yes. What's up?**

Ema: **something I saw in the woods at Bat Lady's. I think we should take a closer look.**

Now? I thought, but then again, when would it be a better time? We needed the cover of dark, I guess, because I wasn't sure we could approach the yard during the day without being seen. I threw on a pair of sweats, grabbed a flashlight, and headed for the front door.

When I reached for the knob, I heard a voice behind me say, "Where are you going?"

It was Myron. "Out," I said.

He made a production of looking at his watch. "It's late."

"I know."

"And it's a school night."

I hated when my uncle tried to play parent. "Thanks for the heads-up. I shouldn't be gone long."

"I think you should tell me where you're going."

"I'm just meeting a friend," I said, hoping that would end it. No such luck.

"Is it that Rachel girl who was here earlier?" my uncle asked.

I needed to nip this in the bud. "We had a deal when I agreed to stay here," I said. "Part of that was, you were going to stay out of my business."

"I never agreed to let you go out at all hours."

"Yeah, you kind of did. I'm just meeting a friend. It's not a big deal."

I rushed out before he could argue. I knew that Myron was trying to do the right thing here, but man, he was the wrong guy to try. I found Ema about a block away from Bat Lady's house.

"How do you get out so late?" I asked her.

"What?"

"You're fourteen years old and you're out at all hours," I said. "Don't your parents get mad?"

Ema frowned. "Are you writing my biography or something?"

I frowned right back. "Good one."

"Yeah, sorry, that was pretty lame."

"Writing your biography."

"I know," she said. "I used to be funnier. I mean, before I hung out with you."

We both slowly turned and looked down the street at Bat Lady's house. In a word: spooky. It was nearly midnight now. The house was totally dark, except for one light on, shining from an upstairs corner window. Her bedroom, I guessed. Shouldn't an old lady have all the lights out by now? What was Bat Lady doing up there at this hour? I imagined her alone, lying in bed, reading or casting spells or devouring small children.

Man, I had to get a grip.

"So what did you want to check out?" I asked Ema.

"When I was hiding in the woods from that bald guy, I spotted something behind the garage."

"What?"

"I don't know exactly." She seemed to think about how to proceed. "It looked like a garden or something. And I thought I saw . . ." Ema stopped, swallowed. "I thought maybe I saw a tombstone."

The air was hot and humid tonight, but I suddenly felt a chill. "You mean, a tombstone like in a grave?"

"I don't know. It might have just been a stone or something. That's why I thought we should check it out."

I agreed. I also wanted to check out the garage. What, I had been wondering, had that car been doing there anyway? If they were just visiting Bat Lady—and I couldn't really fathom that—why not just leave the car outside? Why go to the trouble of putting it in that small garage that barely had room for the one vehicle?

I flashed back to my last encounter with the shaved-head man:

Is my father still alive?

We'll talk.

Dang straight you'll talk. But I wasn't about to sit on my butt and wait for that. We started for the woods behind Bat Lady's house. The flashlights posed a dilemma. Use them and someone might see and call the cops. Don't use them and, well, we couldn't see. For now, Ema and I kept them off, figuring we could turn them on when we got closer.

The streetlights gave off enough illumination for us to reach the edge of the woods. Again I was stunned to see how close the trees came to Bat Lady's back door. The lights were off in her backyard too. I crept up to the kitchen door. Ema whispered, "What are you doing?"

Good question. I wasn't about to break in again, was I? Especially not at night. Still I was drawn to the area. I don't know why. I bent down low and checked the basement windows. Again it was pitch black. Not only that, every shade was pulled down tight. I couldn't see a thing.

I thought about the last time I was here—inside Bat Lady's house. I thought about that old photograph, that same butterfly I saw on the placard by my father's grave. I thought about the light going on in the basement.

What, I wondered, was down there? For that matter, what was upstairs, in that room where the light was still on?

"Mickey?"

It was Ema. "Where's this garden?" I whispered.

"Behind the garage. This way."

We took two steps into the trees and stopped. It was simply too dark. I could barely see my hand in front of my face. We had to risk it. I took out my flashlight and kept the beam low. When we reached the garage, I tried to look inside but there were no windows.

"It's back here," Ema whispered.

I took a quick glance behind me. From the back, all the lights were still out at Bat Lady's house. I wondered if that upstairs bedroom light remained on. Maybe Bat Lady had fallen asleep. Maybe she had fallen asleep hours ago and just forgot to turn off the light. Or maybe she had died and that was why the light was still on.

Nice thought, Mickey!

Ema and I hugged the side of the garage as we felt our way. When we reached the back corner, I shined the flashlight in front of me.

What the . . . ?

Ema had been right. There was a garden. I don't know much about plants or flowers, but I could see this one was well kept and rather stunning. Here, in this mostly green wilderness, was a burst of well-tended color. A foot-high fence surrounded an area that was maybe fifteen feet by fifteen feet. There was a path right down the middle, gorgeous flowers blossoming on either side. And there, at the end of the path, was what definitely looked like a tombstone.

For a moment Ema and I didn't move. Behind me I thought I could hear music now. Faint. Rock music. I looked at Ema. She heard it too. We slowly pivoted toward the Bat Lady's house. The lights were still out. But the music was definitely coming from there.

Ema turned back to the tombstone. "The grave," she said. "It's probably for a pet, right?"

"Right," I said too quickly.

"We should probably take a closer look, though."

"Right," I said again. I could actually feel my legs quaking now. I took the lead. We started toward the little fence and stepped over it. We made our way down the narrow path and stopped in front of the tombstone. I bent down. Ema followed. The music was still faint, but now I was able to make out some lyrics:

My only love,
We'll never see yesterday again. . . .

Rock music. The voice sounded familiar—Gabriel Wire from HorsePower maybe?—but I'd never heard the song before. I shook it off and shined the flashlight onto the worn gray tombstone. For a second—just a split second—I had the weirdest thought that I would see Ashley's name on the tombstone, that someone had killed her and buried her here, and that this was the end of my search. Like I said, the thought only lasted a split second. But it sent shivers everywhere.

The beam from the flashlight hit the top of the tombstone. First observation: the tombstone was old and worn. If it had been for a pet, that animal had died long ago.

I inched the beam down. The second thing I spotted on the tombstone were, well, words. An epitaph, I figured. I read it once, then a second time, and I still wasn't sure what to make of it:

LET US LABOR TO MAKE THE HEART GROW LARGER,
AS WE BECOME OLDER,
AS SPREADING OAK GIVES MORE SHELTER.

"Do you get it?" Ema asked.

The word *shelter* was all in caps. Why? Once again, I thought about my father. I thought about that retirement letter from the Abeona . . .

Shelter.

Coincidence?

I scanned the flashlight lower:

HERE LIES E.S.
A CHILDHOOD LOST FOR CHILDREN

"'A childhood lost for children,'" Ema read out loud. "What the heck does that mean?"

"I don't know."

"Who's E.S.?"

I shook my head again. "Maybe it's her dog or something."

"A dog whose childhood was lost for children?"

Good point. She was right. That made no sense. I lowered the flashlight a little more, almost to the ground. And there in small print:

A30432

I felt my blood go cold.

"How do I know that number?" Ema asked.

"The license plate of the black car."

"Oh. Right." Then she shook her head. "Why the heck is that here?"

I had no idea. "Maybe it's a date," I said.

"A date that starts with the letter *A*?"

"The numbers. Three could stand for March. Fourth day. Nineteen thirty-two."

Ema frowned. "You think?"

In truth, no, I didn't. I stood there baffled while Ema moved around the tombstone, using the light from her cell phone to see. The music still came from the house. It was past midnight.

What kind of old lady plays rock music after midnight?

One who still plays old vinyl records. One who keeps a weird tombstone in her wooded backyard. One who has strange visitors in a black car with a license plate number engraved on that same weird tombstone. One who told a teenage boy that his dead father was still alive.

"What's this?" Ema asked.

I snapped back to the present. "What?"

"Behind here." She was pointing to the back of the tombstone. "There's something carved into the back."

I walked over slowly, but I knew. I just knew. And when I reached the back of the tombstone and shined the light on it, I was barely surprised.

A butterfly with animal eyes on its wings.

Ema gasped. The music in the house stopped. Just like that. Like someone had flicked the off switch the moment my eyes found that dang symbol.

Ema looked up at my face and saw something troubling. "Mickey?"

Nope, there was no surprise. Not anymore. There was rage now. I wanted answers. I was going to get them, no matter what. I wasn't going to wait for Mr. Shaved Head with the British accent to contact me. I wasn't going to wait for Bat Lady to fly down and leave me another cryptic clue. Heck, I wasn't even going to wait until tomorrow.

I was going to find out now.

"Mickey?"

"Go home, Ema."

"What? You're kidding, right?"

I turned and stormed my way back to the house. I pulled out my wallet and started searching for my thin card to open the lock again.

Behind me, Ema asked, "Where are you going?"

"Inside."

"You can't just . . . Mickey?"

I didn't stop. Yes, I was going to break into this house again. I was going to poke around and search that basement—and if I had to climb those stairs and break into Bat Lady's bedroom to get answers, well, I would do that too.

"Mickey, slow down."

"I can't."

Ema grabbed hold of my arm. I turned. "Just take a breath, okay?"

I gently shook off her hold. "That butterfly or whatever the heck it is? It was on a photograph in Bat Lady's house—a photograph that must have been forty or fifty years old. It was on a placard on my father's grave. I'm not waiting, Ema. I need to get some answers now."

I reached the back door and prepared my credit card. I tried to slide it in the crack, just like last time.

No go.

There was a new lock, new doorknob, and what looked like steel enforcements in the door. I looked back at Ema.

"That was fast," she said. "Now what?"

"Now you leave," I said.

She faked a yawn. "No, I don't think that's going to happen."

I shrugged. "Okay. You asked for it."

When I knocked on the door, Ema actually gasped out loud and took two steps back.

There was no answer. I pressed my ear against the door and listened. No sound. I pounded harder. No answer. I pounded harder still, and now I added a shout.

"Hello? Bat Lady? Open up! Open up right now!"

Ema tried to stop me. "Mickey?"

I ignored her. I kicked the door. I hit it again with my fists. I didn't care. Add all the steel enforcements you liked. I was getting inside and I was getting answers.

Then a giant beam of light hit me from the side.

I know beams don't "hit" you, but that's how it felt. The light was so sudden and bright that I actually jumped back, raising my arms like I was warding off an intruder. I heard a *swoosh* to my right and realized that Ema was running away.

A voice shouted, "Don't move!"

I didn't. I didn't know what to do. I wondered if it was my guy with the shaved head, but no, there was no British accent. The light came closer. I heard footsteps behind it. There was more than one guy—maybe two or three.

"Uh, could you lower the beam?" I asked.

The light stayed right on my face, moving closer and closer. I shut my eyes. I wondered whether I should just run. I didn't know who this was. I was fast. I could get away, right? But then I thought about Ema. If I ran, whoever this is might have heard her and take chase. They might catch her. This way, with him focusing solely on me, Ema would be safest.

"Don't move," he said again, only a few yards away now.

As he took another step, I heard the sound of a radio or walkie-talkie. There was static. Then two men talking. I heard more of the radios behind him. Another light shone on me.

"Well, well," the voice said. "Look what we got here. Is this another attempted break-in, Mickey?"

I recognized the voice now. Police Chief Taylor. Troy's father.

"I wasn't breaking in," I said. "I was knocking."

"Sure you were. And what's the card in your hand?"

Uh-oh.

Another cop came over to him. "Need help, Chief?"

"Oh, I think I got this one under control. Turn around and put your hands behind your back."

I did as he asked. I guess I should have been expecting it, but suddenly I felt the snap of handcuffs on me. Chief Taylor leaned in close and whispered, "Heard you jumped my boy when he wasn't looking."

"You heard wrong," I said. "He just got his butt kicked for picking on the wrong underclassman."

Chief Taylor pulled on my arms a little too hard. Pain shot up my shoulders. He led me around front. I saw two cop cars. We started toward them. The back door opened. Chief Taylor put his hand on my head and pushed me in. I looked back at Bat Lady's house, up at the window where the bedroom light still shone.

The curtain moved—and suddenly, Bat Lady's face appeared.

I almost screamed out loud.

Somehow, even from this distance, even through the back window of the police cruiser, I could see that she was looking directly at me, directly into my eyes. Her mouth was moving. She kept saying the same thing over and over again, like a mantra. I watched her while Chief Taylor got in the front seat of the cruiser. Bat Lady kept mouthing the same words to me. I tried to make them out.

The car started up. We pulled away from the curb. Bat Lady's mouthing got more urgent now, as if she was trying to reach me before I vanished from sight. And as she did, as she mouthed the two words yet again, I thought that maybe I had figured out those two words, the two words that Bat Lady was trying so desperately to tell me:

"Save Ashley."

chapter 15

MYRON GOT ME OUT.

I sat in a holding cell. The cop who unlocked the barred door looked sheepish, as if he couldn't believe Chief Taylor had actually stuck me in there. Myron approached as though he wanted to hug me, but my body language must have warned him that it'd be the wrong move. He gave my shoulder a quick pat instead.

"Thank you," I mumbled.

Myron nodded. On our way out, Chief Taylor blocked our path. Myron sort of pushed me behind him, taking the lead. He and Taylor stared each other down for what seemed like an eternity. I remembered my last run-in with the police chief, at the Kents' house: *"Smart mouth. Just like your uncle."*

"Now that your nephew has an adult with him," Taylor finally said, "I'd like to ask him some questions."

"About what?" Myron asked.

I could not only see the dislike between the two men—I could actually feel it.

"There was a break-in at the Kent household. Your nephew was found in the immediate area of that crime. We want to ask him about that—as well as about tonight's attempted break-in."

"Break-in," Myron repeated.

"Yes."

"Where he knocked on a door and never even entered the residence."

"I said *attempted* break-in. He was also trespassing."

"No," Myron said, "he wasn't. He was knocking on a door."

"Don't tell me the law."

Myron just shook his head and started for the door. Taylor got in his way again. "Where are you going? I thought I made it clear I wanted to ask your nephew some questions."

"He isn't talking to you."

"Says who?"

"Says his attorney."

Chief Taylor looked at Myron as if he were something that had just dropped out of a dog's behind. "Oh, that's right. After you blew your basketball career, you became a scum-sucking lawyer."

Myron just grinned at him. "We'll be on our way."

"That's the way you're going to play? Then I'm going to have to charge him. Maybe hold him overnight."

Myron looked behind him. Two other cops stood in the doorway. They had their eyes downcast. This wasn't the way they wanted to play this either.

"Go ahead," Myron said. "You'll get laughed out of court."

"You really want to go that route?" Taylor asked.

No, I thought.

"What my nephew did isn't a crime." Myron moved a little closer to Chief Taylor. "You know what was a crime, though, Eddie?"

Chief Taylor—I guess his first name was Eddie—said nothing.

"That time you egged my house junior year," Myron said. "Remember that, Eddie? The cops picked you up, but they didn't haul your dumb ass into the station like this. They drove you home. Or that time Chief Davis caught you breaking beer bottles against the school. Big tough guy, breaking bottles, until Davis drove up. Remember how you cried like a baby—"

"Shut up!"

"—when he threatened to put you in the squad car?" Myron turned to me. "Mickey, did you cry?"

I shook my head.

"Well, Chief Taylor did. Like a three-year-old. Ah yes, I remember it like it was yesterday. You cried—"

Taylor was the red of a sports car. "Shut up!"

The other two cops were snickering.

"But even then Chief Davis just drove you home," Myron went on. "He didn't cuff you. He didn't drag you in because he had an old beef with your uncle, which, really, is such a cowardly thing to do."

Taylor caught his breath. "You think that's what this is?"

Myron stepped closer. "I know that's what this is."

"Take a step back, Myron."

"Or?"

"Do you want to make an enemy of the chief of police?"

"It seems," Myron said, maneuvering me around Taylor and starting us for the exit, "I already have."

We headed to the parking lot without speaking. When we got into the car, Myron said, "Did you do anything against the law?"

"No."

"You asked me about Bat Lady's house. Then you paid her a late-night visit."

I didn't reply.

"Anything you want to tell me about?" Myron asked.

I thought about it. "No, not right now."

Myron nodded. "Okay then."

That was all. He didn't ask more questions. He started up the car, and we drove home in silence that was, for a change, somewhat comfortable.

. . .

That night, when the dream starts, my father is still alive.

He has a basketball in his hand and he's smiling at me.

"Hey, Mickey."

"Dad?"

He nods.

I feel such happiness, such hope. I am nearly crying with joy. I rush over to him, but suddenly he isn't there anymore. He is behind me. I run after him again, and again he vanishes. I start to get it now. I start to get that this might be a dream and when I wake up, my father will be dead again. Panic takes hold. I move faster. I jump closer to him, and I manage to get my arms around him. I embrace him with everything I have, and for a moment, he feels so real that I think, no, wait, this is reality! He is alive! He never died!

But even as I think that, I can start to feel my grip slipping. Behind him, I see that paramedic with the sandy hair and the green eyes. He is giving me that same heavy look. I yell, "No," and hug my dad harder, dig my face right into his chest. I start to cry onto his favorite blue shirt. But my dad is fading away now. His smile is gone.

"No!" I shout again.

I close my eyes and hold on tighter, but it doesn't do any good. It's like trying to hold on to smoke. The dream is ending. I can see consciousness making its way in.

"Please don't leave me," I say out loud.

I woke up in Myron's basement, sweating and panting. I put my hand to my face and could still feel the tears there. I swallowed hard and got out of bed.

I took a shower and headed to school. Rachel and I worked on our project some more during Mrs. Friedman's class. At one point, Rachel asked, "What's wrong?"

"Nothing. Why?"

"That was like your fifth yawn."

"Sorry."

"A girl could get a complex," she said.

"It's not the company," I said. "Just a bad night's sleep."

She looked at me with those big blue eyes. Her skin was flawless. I wanted to reach out and touch her face. "Can I ask you something personal?" she asked.

I gave her a half nod.

"Why do you live with your uncle?"

"You mean, why don't I live with my parents?"

"Yes."

I kept my eyes on the desk, on a smug picture of Robespierre from early 1794. I wonder if the smug Robespierre had any inkling what the next few months would bring. "My mother is in rehab," I said. "My father is dead."

"Oh," she said, her hand coming up to her mouth. "I'm sorry. I didn't mean to intrude or . . ."

Her voice just sort of faded away. I lifted my head and managed a smile.

"It's okay," I said.

"Is that what you dreamed about? Your mom and dad?"

"My dad," I said, surprising myself.

"Can I ask how he died?"

"A car crash."

"Is that what you dreamed about?"

Enough, I thought. But then I said, "I was there."

"At the car crash?"

"Yes."

"You were in the car?"

I nodded.

"Were you hurt?"

I had broken ribs and spent three weeks in the hospital. But that pain was nothing compared to the vision of watching my father die. "A little," I said.

"What happened?"

I could still see it. The two of us in the car, laughing, the radio on, the sudden jar of the crash, the snap of the head, the blood, the sirens. I woke up trapped, unable to move. I could see the paramedic with the sandy blond hair working on my too-still father. I was trapped in the seat next to him, the fireman working to free me with the Jaws of Life, and then the sandy-haired paramedic looked up at me; and I remember his green eyes with the yellow circle around the pupil—and the eyes seemed to say that nothing would ever be the same.

"Hey, it's okay," Rachel said with the most gentle voice. "We're history partners—it doesn't mean you have to bare your soul. Okay?"

I nodded gratefully as the bell rang, chasing away that image of the sandy-haired paramedic with the green eyes. At lunch, Ema and I filled Spoon in on our late-night visit to Bat Lady's house. He looked hurt.

"You didn't invite me?"

"It was like two in the morning," I said. "We figured you'd be asleep."

"Me? I'm an up-all-night party animal."

"Right," Ema said. "By the way, do your jammies have feetsies?"

Spoon frowned. "Tell me that epitaph again."

Ema handed Spoon her phone. She had snapped a picture of it with her cell phone camera:

LET US LABOR TO MAKE THE HEART GROW LARGER,
AS WE BECOME OLDER,
AS SPREADING OAK GIVES MORE SHELTER.

Two minutes later, Spoon said, "It's a quote from Richard Jefferies, a nineteenth-century English nature writer noted for his depiction of English rural life in essays, books of natural history, and novels."

We looked at him.

"What? I just Googled the quote and read his bio on Wikipedia. There is nothing on that childhood lost for children quote, so I don't know what that's about, but I can do more research later."

"Good idea," I said.

"Why don't we all meet after school and go to the library?" Ema suggested. "We can see what we can find out about Bat Lady from the town archives too."

"I can't today," I said.

"Oh?"

"I have a basketball game," I said.

I didn't want to go into detail. I had a plan. I would go down on the bus to Newark like I did most days. I might even play a little with Tyrell and the gang. Then, with Ema and Spoon safe here in town, I would visit Antoine LeMaire at the address near the Plan B Go-Go Lounge.

So that was what I did. As soon as school ended, I walked to the bus stop on Northfield Avenue and hopped on the number 164. First, I took out my cell phone. I had one picture of Ashley, dressed in her prim sweater, her smile shy. I made it my default screen so if I needed to show it to anyone, I would have it at the ready.

There was a light mist of rain, so we had fewer guys show up for pickup basketball. Tyrell wasn't there. One of the other guys told me that he was studying for some big test at school. We started playing, but the rain kicked in, so we called it off. I changed back into my school clothes, and using the directions I'd gotten online, I started to walk over to Antoine LeMaire's address.

The rain was coming down hard now. I didn't mind. I like rain. I was born in a small village in the Chiang Mai province in northern Thailand. My parents were helping out one of the hill tribes called the Lisu. The shaman—the sorcerer, medicine man, one who acts as a medium between the visible world and the spirit world—gave my father a list of things I must do during my lifetime. One was to "dance naked in the rain." I don't know why I've always liked that one, but I do. I've done it, though not recently, but ever since I was old enough to understand the list, I have always had a funny appreciation for the rain.

When I arrived at the address, I was surprised to see that it wasn't a residence near the Plan B Go-Go Lounge—it *was* the Plan B Go-Go Lounge. I looked for an apartment on the top, but there was only the lounge entrance. A huge black man stood in front of it. There was a frayed velvet rope and a big pink-once-red awning. On the awning was a silhouette of a voluptuous woman. The door was blacked-out glass with faded lettering. A sign read: **50 LIVE BEAUTIFUL GO-GO SHOWGIRLS—AND TWO UGLY DEAD ONES**.

Funny.

The huge man—a bouncer—frowned at me and pointed to another weathered sign: **NO ONE UNDER 21 PERMITTED**.

I was going to ask the bouncer whether he knew Antoine LeMaire, but that seemed like the wrong move. I took out my wallet and produced the fake Robert Johnson ID saying I was twenty-one. He looked at it, looked at me, knew it was probably a fake, didn't much care. It was five P.M., but business was brisk. Men entered and left in drifts and waves.

There were all kinds—jeans and flannel shirts, sneakers and work boots, suits and ties and shined shoes. Some fist-bumped the bouncer as they came and went.

"Thirty-dollar cover charge," the bouncer said to me.

Wow. "Thirty dollars just to enter?"

The big man nodded. "Includes buffet dinner. Tonight is Tex-Mex."

I made a face at the thought. He let me through. I pushed open the door and was greeted by darkness. It took a few seconds for my eyes to adjust. A bikini-clad woman/girl who looked about my age stood by a cash register. I gave her thirty dollars. She handed me a plate, barely looking up at me. "For the buffet," she said by way of explanation. "That way." She pointed to the curtain on the right.

I looked at the plate. It was white with the same voluptuous silhouette as on the awning, plus the rather obvious slogan: *Plan B—Where You Go When Plan A Doesn't Work Out.*

My mouth felt dry. My step slowed. I will make a confession to you now. I was nervous, but I was also, well, I was curious. I had never been in a place like this. I realize I should be above that and be mature about it and all that, but a part of me felt pretty naughty and a part of me kind of liked that.

The music was loud with a driving beat. The first thing I passed was an ATM that let you get your cash in fives, tens, or twenties. This, I could see, was to tip the dancers. Men hung at a stage-bar, mostly drinking beer, while the women danced in stiletto heels so high they doubled as stilts. I tried not to stare. Some of the dancers were indeed beautiful. Some were not. I watched them work the men for tips. A sign read: **YOUR STAY HERE IS TOUCH AND GO—TOUCH AND YOU GO**. Despite that, the men jammed the paper money into G-strings with little hesitation.

Behind me was the buffet. I took a quick glance. The chips were Doritos. The ground beef was marinating in so much lard it looked as if it were encased in Jell-O. The whole place, even in the dark, felt more than looked dirty. I wasn't a germaphobe, but even without the warning, I didn't want to "touch" anything.

So now what?

I found an empty booth in a dark corner. Seconds after I sat down, two women approached me. The one with the plunging neckline and fire-engine-red dye job slid next to me. It was hard to tell her age. Could be a hard twenty-year-old or an okay thirty or a good forty. I bet on the youngest. The other woman was a waitress.

The fire-engine redhead who sat down smiled at me. She tried her best to make the smile real, but she couldn't hide the fact that it was an act, that it was like someone had just painted it on her face. None of it reached her wary eyes. It was a bright, wide smile and yet one of the saddest I had ever seen.

"I'm Candy," she said to me.

"I'm M—uh, Bob," I said. "I'm Bob."

"You sure?"

"Yep. Bob."

"You're adorable."

"Thanks," I said.

Even when I'm nervous, even in a place like this, I still know how to deliver the smooth lines.

Candy leaned forward a little, making sure to offer a peek. "Buy me a drink?"

I didn't quite get it, so I said, "Huh? I mean, I guess."

"This your first time here?"

"Yes," I said. "I just turned twenty-one."

"That's sweet. See, it's customary to buy a drink for yourself and one for me. We could just split a bottle of champagne."

"How much would that cost?"

The smile flickered when I asked that.

The waitress said, "Three hundred dollars plus tip."

I was in a booth, which was good—if I was in a chair, I would have fallen off it.

"Um, how about if we both have Diet Cokes?" I asked. "How much is that?"

Now the smile was all the way gone. Clearly I was no longer adorable.

"Twenty dollars plus tip."

That would pretty much clear me out, but I nodded. The waitress left me alone with Candy. She was studying me now. Then she asked, "Why are you here?"

"What do you mean?"

"If you had really just turned twenty-one, you'd be here

with friends. You don't look like you really want to be here. So what's your deal?"

So much for working undercover, but maybe this was better anyway. "I'm looking for someone," I said.

"Aren't we all?" Candy replied.

"What?"

She shook her head. "Who you looking for, honey?"

"A man named Antoine LeMaire."

The color drained from her face.

"You know him?"

A look of pure terror came to her. "I have to go."

"Wait," I said, putting my hand on her arm. She pulled away fast and hard, and I remembered the Touch and Go sign. She hurried away. I sat there, not sure what to do. Unfortunately my mind was made up for me. The big bouncer from the entrance was hustling his way over to me. I took out my cell phone, prepared to call someone, anyone, so I'd have a witness, but I wasn't getting service. Terrific.

The big bouncer leaned over me like a lunar eclipse. "Let me see your ID again."

I dug into my pocket and handed it to him.

"You don't look twenty-one," he said.

"That's because it's dark in here. Outside, in the good light, you let me in, so I must have."

His whole being seemed to frown at me. "What are you here for?"

"A good time?" I tried.

"Come with me," he said.

There wasn't much point in arguing. Two other bruisers were lined up a few feet behind him and even on my best day, I couldn't take out all three. Or even one probably. So I stood on shaky legs and headed toward the exit. My visit had failed—or had it? Clearly Antoine LeMaire was around here. Clearly his name struck a chord. So now I could go home and regroup . . .

A giant hand fell on my shoulder as I reached the exit.

"Not so fast," the bouncer said. "This way."

Uh-oh.

Keeping his hand on my shoulder, he steered me down a long corridor. The two other bouncers followed us. I didn't like that. There were posters of "showgirls" on the walls. We passed the bathrooms and two more doors and made a left. There was another door at the end of the corridor. We stopped in front of it.

I didn't like this.

"I'd like to leave," I said.

The bouncer didn't reply. He used a key and unlocked the door. He pushed me in and closed the door behind us. We were in an office of some kind. There was a desk and more photographs of girls on the wall.

"I'd like to leave," I said again.

"Maybe later," the bouncer said.

Maybe?

A door behind the desk opened, and a short, wiry man

entered. His short-sleeved dress shirt was shiny and unbuttoned down to the navel, revealing a host of gold chains and, uh, bling. His arms were knotted, ropy muscle. Have you ever seen someone who gave you the chills just by entering a room? This guy had that. Even the big bouncer, who had to be a foot taller and a hundred pounds heavier than the short guy, took half a step back. A hush fell over us.

The short, wiry man had the narrow face of a ferret and what I can only describe as psycho eyes. I know that you are not supposed to judge people by their looks, but a blind man would be able to see that this guy was serious bad news.

"Hello there," he said to me. "My name is Buddy Ray. What's yours?" He had a faint lisp.

I swallowed. "Robert Johnson."

Buddy Ray's smile would make small children flee to their mamas. "Nice to meet you, Robert."

Buddy Ray—I didn't know if that was a double first name or a first and last name—looked me over as though I were a bite-size snack. Something was off with this guy—you could just see it. He kept licking his lips. I risked a glance back at the big bouncer. Even he looked jittery in Buddy Ray's presence.

As Buddy Ray approached, a pungent stench of cheap cologne failing to mask foul body odor wafted off him, the foul smell taking the lead like a Doberman he was walking. Buddy Ray stopped directly in front of me, maybe six inches away. I held my breath and stood my ground. I, too, had a foot on him. The bouncer took another step backward.

Buddy Ray craned his neck up at me and renewed the smile. Then, without warning, he punched me hard and deep in the stomach. I doubled over, the air whooshing out of me. I fell to my knees, gasping for air, but none would come. It felt as though a giant hand were holding my face underwater. I couldn't breathe. My entire body started craving oxygen, just one breath, but I couldn't get it. I dropped all the way to the floor, curled up in a fetal position.

Buddy Ray stood over me. The psycho eyes had lit up like something in a video game. His voice, when he spoke, was soft. "Tell me what you know about Antoine LeMaire."

I gulped but still no air would come. My lungs ached.

Buddy Ray kicked me in the ribs with the toe of his cowboy boot.

I rolled away, the pain from the kick barely registering because I still couldn't draw air. That was all I could think about. Breathing. Every cell in my body yearned for oxygen. I just needed time to gather one breath.

Buddy Ray turned to his big bouncer. "Pick him up, Derrick."

"He's just a kid, Buddy Ray."

"Pick him up."

Air. I finally managed to gulp down a few breaths. Derrick's big hands bunched up my shirt near the shoulders. He lifted me as if I were a light load of laundry.

"Pin his arms back," Buddy Ray said.

I could tell Derrick didn't like it, but he did as he was told.

He laced his massive arms through mine and pulled back so that my stomach and chest were totally exposed. He tightened his grip, locking me in place. I could feel the tendons ripping across my shoulder sockets. Buddy Ray was still licking his lips, enjoying this way too much.

"Please," I said as soon as I could gather enough air to speak. "I don't know Antoine LeMaire. I'm looking for him too."

Buddy Ray studied my face. "Is your name really Robert Johnson?"

I didn't know how to answer that one.

He reached into my pocket and took out my cell phone. "I bet this will give us your real name and home address." Another smile. "So Derrick and I can visit you whenever we like."

I struggled, but that just made Derrick mad. Buddy Ray flicked my cell phone on—and then his face froze. He looked back at me, his face twisted in rage, and then he turned the camera in my direction.

It was the picture of Ashley.

Buddy Ray's body started quaking. "Where is she?"

"I don't know."

"You're lying to me," he said, keeping his voice low. "Where. Is. She?"

"That's why I'm here. I'm looking for her."

"So you're here for Antoine?"

"I'm here," I said, "for me."

Buddy Ray took a few deep breaths, and I didn't like what I was seeing on his face. He looked at Derrick. "We should take him to the dungeon."

The dungeon?

Even Derrick looked shell-shocked when he said that. "I don't know, boss."

Buddy Ray turned back to me. "Here's what's going to happen," Buddy Ray said to me, again his voice a quiet lisp. "With Derrick holding you in place, I'm going to sock you in the gut again. Harder this time. Then, much as you're going to want to bend and fall back on the floor, Derrick is going to hold you up. And then, if you don't talk, we will take you to the dungeon."

The fear on my face made his grin widen. "Wait," I said. "I don't know anything."

"Maybe, maybe not. But really, I should be sure, right?"

I started to buck, but Derrick held me firm. Buddy Ray took his time, milking the moment. He licked his lips some more and then he took out a pair of brass knuckles.

I shuddered.

Derrick said, "Uh, Buddy Ray?"

"Just hold him."

Buddy Ray slipped on the brass knuckles and slowly made a fist. He showed it to me, like it was something I might want to study before he unleashed it. I didn't know what to do. I tried to tighten my stomach muscles, but really, how would that help? Then, with the maniacal grin at its widest, Buddy

Ray began to cock back his fist. He was just about to let it go when the door behind him, the one he had come through a minute ago, opened. A bikini-clad dancer entered.

"Buddy Ray?" she said.

"Get out!"

It was now or never.

As I mentioned before, I had been trained in combat. In most martial arts schools, you are taught how to punch or chop or kick, how to grapple or use holds or escape them. But for the most part, a fight is about the early tactics. It is about distraction and camouflage and surprise and timing. The girl opening the door had shifted attention away from me for a brief second.

So I had to strike now.

Derrick the bouncer still had me in a killer grip, but we were nearly the same height. I bent my neck forward, tucking my chin to my chest, and then snapped my head back with all my might. The back of my skull landed on his nose like a bowling ball. I heard a crunching sound, like someone stepping on a dried bird's nest.

Derrick cried out and let me go. I didn't bother with a follow-up blow. No need. It was more important that I didn't stay still. No hesitation. There was an open door where the dancer still stood. Moving with everything I had—moving before Buddy Ray could react or Derrick could recover—I leaped over the desk, snatching my phone away from a still-shocked Buddy Ray, and sprinted toward the open door.

No hesitation.

The dancer was in my way. That meant having to run her over, if I had to. A second lost could be the difference between making it out and getting caught. I didn't want to hurt her, but there was simply not enough room to get by. Luckily for both of us, she saw me coming and slid to the right.

I dived through the door and into what might be called a dressing room. There were costumes and boas and lots of dancers crowded in front of one mirror. I expected them to shriek or something like that when I broke through, but they barely looked up.

"Stop him!"

It was Buddy Ray.

I kept moving, running across the dressing room, banging through another door, and finding myself . . .

. . . onstage?

The patrons looked surprised to see me onstage. Then again, so did I. One of the men cupped his hands into a flesh megaphone and yelled, "Boo!" The other men joined in. I was about to jump down, but now I saw the other two bouncers rushing toward me. I turned back, but Buddy Ray was there, Derrick following, holding his nose. Blood leaked through his fingers.

Trapped.

Distraction, camouflage, surprise, timing.

I stayed onstage and ran down it, kicking every beer bottle I could. I didn't have a plan other than to create a distraction to the point of chaos. The dancers onstage screamed. The patrons started jumping back, crashing into one another, pushing and shoving. It wouldn't take much. You have a room filled with inebriated, frustrated men who were spending too much money on what really, in the end, was a pretty pathetic Plan B. Testosterone flowed like the watered-down drinks.

Fights started breaking out.

I leaped off the stage, hurdling a group of men. I landed on one, rolled off him, kept moving. The sea of humanity behind me provided a wall. Buddy Ray and the bouncers were trying to get through to me. I turned and looked for an exit.

Nothing.

Buddy Ray and the bouncers were getting closer. I was cornered again.

"Psst, this way."

I spotted the fire-engine-red hair first. It was Candy. She had ducked under a table. I got down on my hands and knees and started crawling toward her.

Someone grabbed my ankle.

I didn't bother to look. I kicked out with my foot, mule-like, and somehow I pulled away. I crawled faster, following Candy on all fours. She opened a half door, like an escape hatch, and slid through it. Again I followed her. She was already up on the other side. She helped me to my feet.

"This way."

We were in a blue room with tons of throw pillows on the floor and a small round stage with a pole in the center. I heard a noise behind us and started for the nearest door. Candy put her hand out to stop me.

"Don't," she said with a shudder. "That leads to the dungeon. You don't ever want to go down there."

She didn't have to tell me twice. I had no interest in visiting the dungeon, thank you very much. I signaled for her to lead the way. We hurried to the other side of the room and pushed against a heavy metal fire door.

I was outside!

Candy grabbed my arm. "You don't work for Antoine, do you?"

"No," I said. I held up my phone. "I'm trying to find this girl."

Candy gasped. There was no doubt—she recognized Ashley.

"You know her," I said.

"Ashley," Candy said. "She was so special, so smart. She was my only friend here."

Was?

"Where is she?" I asked.

"She's gone," Candy said in the saddest of voices. "Once you get into Antoine's van, you're gone forever."

There was a commotion coming from the other side of the door. Buddy Ray and the bouncers weren't far away.

"Run!" Candy said.

"Wait. What do you mean, she's gone?"

"No time."

"I have to know."

Candy put her hands on my chest, grabbing my shirt. "Antoine LeMaire got her months ago. The White Death. There's nothing you can do for Ashley. She's gone, just like the others. All you can do now is save yourself."

I shook my head. "She goes to my high school. She was fine last week."

Candy looked puzzled, but now there was more noise coming closer. "Run!" she shouted, pushing me away as she ran down the alley. "Just run and don't come back!"

I took off in the other direction, toward the street, running hard and fast.

I didn't stop until I was back at the bus station, back on the 164 heading home.

chapter 16

UNCLE MYRON WASN'T HOME.

That was fine with me. I looked at my hands. They were
still shaking. I had no idea what to do. I couldn't tell him—
what would I say? See, I sneaked into this go-go bar with a
fake ID, and then, well, the bouncer and some guy named
Buddy Ray assaulted me. . . . Right, sure. Who'd buy that? I
didn't have a mark on me. Buddy Ray and the big bouncer
would probably both swear that they threw me out when
they realized that my ID was fake.

No, that wasn't the answer.

Candy's words kept echoing in my head. *There's nothing
you can do for Ashley. She's gone, just like the others.*

I had no idea what she meant by that. Or by the fact that
Antoine LeMaire "got her months ago. The White Death."

Ashley had been in school. She had smiled and laughed and been so wonderfully shy and—and hadn't Candy said that Ashley was her only friend?

What was going on?

One thing was clear. Ashley had secrets. Candy did indeed know her. Worse—a lot worse—so did Buddy Ray.

So now what?

I didn't know. What had I really learned here? Not much. The answer, it seemed, still came down to Antoine LeMaire. I had to find him. But that raised a few questions. Most obvious: How? I didn't think it best to go back to the Plan B. Maybe I could hang around and run some kind of surveillance, but really, was that going to work? And that led to my second question: When I find Antoine—the White Death?—then what do I do?

I started boiling water for pasta, my mind still trying to take it all in. Something played at the edges—something I couldn't quite see yet. But it was there. I sat by myself at the kitchen table. My stomach still hurt from that punch. It would be sore tomorrow.

That niggling in the back of my brain picked up steam. I got the laptop and booted it up. I wanted to take another look at my buddy Antoine LeMaire at Ashley's locker. I watched the tape. Antoine opens the locker, looks inside, sees it's empty, gets upset. I watched the tape again. Then I realized what was bothering me.

The locker was already empty.

Antoine had hoped to find something inside the locker—but whatever it was, it was already gone. That probably meant that Ashley herself had cleared it out. I wondered when. And more than that, I wondered if I could see that moment, if I could see exactly when she had last been in the school. If she had cleared out her locker, it goes to figure that she'd planned to run—that she hadn't met up with foul play or the White Death or whatever other horrible thing could happen to a girl who had some connection to the Plan B Go-Go Lounge.

It stood to reason that Ashley had emptied out the locker and was on the run.

Or did it?

I called Spoon. He picked up on the first ring. I expected him to open up with one of his crazy non sequiturs. But he surprised me.

"Did you find Antoine?" Spoon asked.

"What?"

"You must think Ema and I are morons. A basketball game? Please."

I had to smile at that. "I didn't find him."

"So what happened?"

"I'll tell you tomorrow. In the meantime I have a favor." I told him what I wanted—my theory on Ashley's last visit to the locker being important.

"Hmm," Spoon said, "we don't know when Ashley was last at the locker."

"No."

"And it could have been during the school day."

"Could have been."

He considered that. "I guess we could hit speed reverse and see if we can come up with something. Assuming I can get into the security files again."

"Do you mind?"

"I'm all about the danger."

Spoon hung up. Three minutes later, Ema called me. "Have you eaten yet?" she asked me.

"I'm boiling water now."

"Do you know Baumgart's?"

I did. It was Uncle Myron's favorite restaurant. "I do."

"Meet me there."

There was something funny in her voice, something I hadn't heard before. "I didn't find Antoine."

"Spoon told me. But that's not what I want to talk to you about."

"What's up?"

"I did some research on that tombstone."

"And?"

"And something is really wrong here, Mickey."

Half a century ago, Baumgart's was a Jewish deli and old-fashioned soda fountain—the kind of place where Dad might order a pastrami on rye while the kids sat at the Formica counter and twirled on stools while waiting for a root beer float. Sometime in the 1980s, a gourmet Chinese chef bought the place. Rather than alienate his base, he simply added to it. He kept all the Jewish deli and soda fountain touches and then added nouvelle Chinese to the menu. It made for an intriguing hybrid. Since then, three more Baumgart's had opened up in various New Jersey locales.

Ema sat in a corner booth nursing a chocolate milk shake. I sat with her and ordered one too. The waitress asked whether we wanted something to eat. We both nodded. Ema ordered the peanut noodles, Myron's favorite, and something called sizzle duck crepe. I went with Kung Pao chicken.

"So," she said, "what happened when you went after Antoine LeMaire?"

"Why don't you go first?"

She played with the straw in her milk shake. "I still need time to wrap my head around this." Ema took a sip and leaned back. "By the way, do me a favor: if you want to play overprotective daddy with me, just say so."

"Okay," I said.

"Don't lie."

"You're right. I'm sorry."

"Good," Ema said. "So what happened with Antoine?"

I told her about my visit to the Plan B Go-Go Lounge. The waitress came and brought our food, but neither one of us noticed. When I finished, Ema said, "I won't even bother with the 'whoa.' This is beyond whoa. It's like whoa on steroids. It's like whoa raised to the tenth power."

The smell of Kung Pao chicken rose up from the plate and

suddenly I realized that I was starving. I grabbed my fork and started digging in.

"So," Ema said, "you think, what, your prim and proper Ashley danced in a go-go bar?"

I shrugged mid-bite. "So what did you learn about that tombstone?"

Her face lost a little color. "It's about Bat Lady."

I waited. She hesitated.

"Ema?"

"Yes?"

"When Chief Taylor was dragging me away, I saw Bat Lady in the window. She was trying to tell me something."

Ema's eyes narrowed.

"I can't swear to it," I said, "but I think she was telling me to save Ashley. I know that makes no sense. But whatever it is, whatever you've learned, I need to hear it."

She nodded. "We already know about that Jefferies quote, right?"

"Right."

"So I searched the other stuff. That line about a childhood lost for children."

"And?"

"I found nothing on that exact quote, but I did find this website on . . ." She stopped, shook her head as if she couldn't believe that she was about to go on. "On the Holocaust."

I stopped with my fork half in the air. "As in Nazis and World War Two?"

"Yes."

"I don't understand."

"It was a reference to some of the Jewish children who joined the underground resistance in Poland. See, some of the kids who escaped the death camps lived in the forest. They fought the Nazis in secret. Kids. They would also smuggle goods into the Lodz ghetto, for example. Sometimes, when they could, they even rescued kids heading toward Auschwitz, the Nazis' biggest and most notorious concentration camp."

I just sat there and waited. Ema picked up her milk shake and took a deep long sip. "I still don't understand," I said. "What does this have to do with the tombstone in Bat Lady's garden?"

"You've heard of Anne Frank, right?"

I had, of course. I had not only read *The Diary of Anne Frank*, but when I was twelve, my parents took me to the house in Amsterdam where she hid from the Nazis. The two parts I remember best: One, the moveable bookcase that hid the stairs up to the secret attic where the Frank family stayed. Two, the Anne Frank quote you see as you leave this somber memorial: "Despite everything, I believe that people are really good at heart."

"Of course, I've heard of her," I said.

"There was another girl. A thirteen-year-old Polish girl named Lizzy Sobek who escaped from Auschwitz and worked for the resistance."

The name rang a bell. "I remember reading something about her."

"Me too. We talked a little about her in eighth-grade history. Lizzy Sobek's family was slaughtered in Auschwitz, but somehow she escaped. She is credited with saving hundreds of lives. In one documented case, Lizzy ran a February raid that slowed down a cargo train loaded with Jews heading for the death camps. More than fifty people escaped into the snowy woods—almost all under the age of fifteen. And some of those she saved claim"—Ema stopped, took a deep breath—"that when they escaped, they saw butterflies."

I swallowed. "Butterflies?"

She nodded. "In February. In Poland. Butterflies. Hundreds of them leading them to safety."

I just sat there.

"Lizzy Sobek became known as the Butterfly."

I may have been shaking my head, but I can't swear to it. I knew that we were both thinking the same thing. Butterfly—like on those T-shirts in the old photograph, at my father's gravesite, on the tombstone in Bat Lady's backyard. It couldn't be a coincidence.

"Lizzy Sobek," I said—and suddenly my blood went cold again. "Lizzy could be short for Elizabeth."

"It was," Ema said.

Elizabeth Sobek. E.S. The initials on that tombstone. Another coincidence? I asked the obvious question: "What became of Lizzy Sobek?"

"That's the thing," Ema said. "No one really knows. The vast majority of scholars believe that she was captured during a raid to free a group of children starving to death near Lodz. They believe that she and other resistance fighters were shot and buried in a mass grave, probably in 1944. But there has never been any proof."

"A childhood lost for children," I said. "That phrase makes more sense now."

Ema nodded. "There's more."

I waited. The restaurant was bustling. People coming and going, enjoying their food, laughing or texting or whatever it is people do at restaurants. But for us, they were gone now. The room was just this booth—just Ema and me and the ghost of some brave, long-dead girl named Lizzy Sobek.

"I did all kinds of searches on those numbers—the ones on the bottom of the tombstone and on that license plate," Ema said. "The A30432. But I came up with nothing."

I sat very still. If she had ended up with nothing, there wouldn't be tears in her eyes.

"So I read more about Lizzy Sobek," Ema said, reaching into her pocket and pulling out a piece of paper. "I found one of those Q and A sites on her life." She unfolded the paper and slid it across the table.

I took it from her. Ema looked off. I turned my attention to the paper:

Question 8: What was Lizzy Sobek's concentration camp tattoo ID number?

It remains unknown. Most people mistakenly believe that every person in a Nazi concentration camp was tattooed, but in truth, the Auschwitz concentration camp complex (including Auschwitz 1, Auschwitz-Birkenau, and Monowitz) was the only location in which prisoners were systematically tattooed during the Holocaust. On September 12, 1942, Lizzy, along with her father, Samuel, her mother, Esther, and her brother, Emmanuel, boarded a transport to Auschwitz-Birkenau. The transport arrived in Auschwitz on September 13, 1942, with 1,121 Jews on board. Men and women were separated. The women selected from this transport, including Lizzy and Esther, were marked with tattoos between the numbers A-30380 and A-30615. Records indicating their exact numbers have not been preserved, so to this day, the number Lizzy Sobek bore on her forearm remains a mystery.

I looked up at Ema and now I had tears in my eyes too. "Have we solved this particular mystery?"

"We may have."

"Which leads to another."

Ema nodded. "How would Bat Lady know the exact same number?"

"And why would she have a tombstone for her in her backyard?"

"Unless . . ."

Ema stopped. We both knew what she was thinking, but I don't think either of us was ready to say it out loud. Maybe we had solved a mystery deeper than a tattoo number. Maybe, after all these years, we had solved the mystery of what really happened to Lizzy Sobek.

chapter 17

THE NEXT MORNING, I called my mother at the Coddington Institute. The operator said, "Please hold."

There were two rings and then the phone was picked up.
"Mickey?"

It wasn't my mother. It was the rehab's director, Christine
Shippee. "I want to talk to my mother."

"And I want to take a shower with Brad Pitt," she said.
"Sorry, I told you, no contact."

"You can't just cut her off from me."

"Uh, yeah, Mickey, I can. Speaking of which, we need to
talk. Do you know what an enabler is?"

Again with that question. "I didn't give her the drugs."

"No, but you're being a candy ass about this. You need to
be tougher on her."

"You don't know what she's been through."

"Sure I do," she said as though stifling a yawn. "Her husband died. Her only son is growing up. She has no prospects. She is scared and lonely and depressed. What, you think your mother's the only one in here with a sob story?"

"Your sympathy," I said, "is overwhelming. No wonder the patients love you."

"I was one of them, Mickey. A manipulative addict. I know how it works. Come by next week and we'll talk more. In the meantime, get to school."

She hung up.

At school, most of the morning was taken up with an assembly program. I don't really remember much of what was being said. Two local politicians tried to "relate" to us, which made for serious condescension and boredom. I spent the time glancing around the room and locking eyes with Rachel.

When lunchtime came, I sat at what was fast becoming our usual table with Ema. Spoon was nowhere to be found. Ema and I tried, for once, to talk about the new movie releases or what music we liked or what TV shows were our favorites—but we kept steering back to the Holocaust and a heroic girl named Lizzy Sobek.

At one point I looked across the room and spotted Troy and Buck. Not surprisingly they smirked at me. Troy had a cocky I-know-something-you-don't-know look on his face and then he started flapping his arms like wings and making an *eek-eek* noise.

"A bat," Ema finally said.

"As in Bat Lady."

"Man, he's clever."

I guessed that his father had told him about my arrest near Bat Lady's house and this was his subtle way of communicating this to us. I responded by pantomiming a yawn. Troy glared when I did that, and then he used his finger to cut across his neck, the international dumbwad sign for, yup, "You're a dead man."

Not worth it. I turned away.

"Do you know where Spoon is?" I asked Ema.

I had caught her mid-chew, so she gestured behind her. Spoon was hurrying over to the table—sprinting really—with an open laptop in his arms. Ms. Owens blocked his path and said, "Walk, don't run."

Spoon nodded and apologized. When he reached us, he was wide-eyed and out of breath. "Shocking," Spoon said.

"What?"

Spoon put the laptop on the table. "Oh boy, you are *so* going to want to see this."

"What is it?" I asked.

He frowned. "Didn't you ask me to check the surveillance video of Ashley's locker?"

"Right."

"Well, I've been going through it since last night. You are not going to believe what I found."

The bell rang. Everyone started for the door, except for the three of us. Spoon sat down in front of the laptop. I pushed my chair over so I was on his immediate right. Ema did likewise so she was on his left.

"Okay," he started, "so I was doing what you asked—checking the video, right? I started with that hooligan breaking into the locker, and then I traveled back from there until I found the last time that Ashley's locker was open."

He stopped, pushed up his glasses.

"And?" I said.

"Watch."

Spoon was about to hit the computer key when Ms. Owens cleared her throat in dramatic fashion.

"The bell rang," she said in a clipped voice.

"We'll be just a minute," I said.

Ms. Owens didn't like that response. "We don't operate on your time, Mr. Bolitar. The bell has sounded. That means you leave the room. You aren't special."

Was she kidding me?

I tried an old standard: "It's schoolwork."

"I don't care if it is a cure for cancer," Ms. Owens said—and on that, I believed her. She slammed the laptop closed, making Spoon gasp out loud. "You had all lunch period to discuss this matter. Move along now or you'll all be in detention."

"You assaulted my laptop," Spoon said.

"Excuse me?"

"You assaulted my battery or whatever they call it."

"Are you challenging my authority, young man?"

Spoon opened his mouth to say more, so I kicked him just hard enough to get him to close it again. I stood, pulling Spoon along with me. The three of us left the cafeteria. In the corridor we quickly discussed what classes we had next. I had English. Spoon had study hall. Ema had "PE, which I'm going to cut anyway."

Spoon rushed us over to a janitor's closet on the lower level. We huddled around the laptop again. Spoon hit the start key and said, "Watch."

And there it was.

Ashley's locker. Spoon had it cued up right where it needed to be—right as the locker was being unlocked. We all watched in silence while the locker was cleaned out, all the possessions dumped into a backpack.

My jaw dropped open.

"I knew it!" Ema said. "I warned you, didn't I?"

It wasn't Ashley clearing out the locker. It wasn't Antoine or Buddy Ray or his big bouncer Derrick. The person who opened up the locker with the combination and cleaned it out was none other than Rachel Caldwell.

First, there was confusion, but that almost immediately gave way to anger.

I was furious. I was beyond furious. I not only felt betrayed, but I felt like the dumbest sort of sap. We get mad at those who hurt or deceive us—we get even madder when they make us feel like fools.

Right now I felt like a great big sucker.

Rachel Caldwell had batted her big blue eyes at me, and I fell for it.

Grab your thesaurus, boys and girls. Sap. Loser. Sucker. Fool. Me!

I played back Rachel's every smile, every coy look, every little laugh.

Phony. All so phony. How had I fallen for her act?

Ema could not have looked more pleased. "I told you that we couldn't trust her."

I said nothing.

Spoon pushed his glasses up. "Whatever you saw on this video doesn't change the main fact."

"What fact is that?" Ema asked.

"That Rachel Caldwell is a first-class, teeth-melting, jaw-dropping, knee-knocking hottie."

Ema rolled her eyes.

The late bell rang. It was time to move. We broke up, Spoon and I going to our respective classes, Ema going . . . wherever it was she was going. I had Mr. Lampf for English. I sat in the back and opened up my notebook, but I can't tell you anything else about the class. I was still consumed by fury. Finally, after some time had passed, I allowed the obvious, more important question to break through my cloud of anger: What could Rachel Caldwell possibly have to do with all this?

I trotted out about a million different scenarios, but none of them made any sense. Logic wasn't working for me, so I let the rage back in. The rage was good right now. The rage reminded me that Rachel Caldwell was in this very building at this very moment. The rage reminded me that I could confront her and then I would find it all out.

When the bell rang, I hurried toward the door. I knew that Rachel had math with Mrs. Cannon right now. I knew that because, well, I just did. Mrs. Cannon's class was only halfway down this same corridor. I often caught glimpses of her in the hallway between this class and the next. Sue me, I looked, okay?

I headed into the corridor and turned right.

There she was. Rachel was turning away from me, her hair seeming to move in perfect slow motion, like in a shampoo ad. I rushed after her, swimming through the throngs of fellow students. She was about to turn the corner when I reached her. I put my hand on her shoulder, maybe a little too roughly. She turned, startled, but when she saw it was me, her face broke into a gorgeous, gut-punching smile.

"Hey, Mickey!" she said as if she couldn't be happier to see me.

Someone should give this girl an Oscar.

"Where's Ashley?"

The smile fell off Rachel's face like an anvil. She tried to get it back, but now it only stayed on in flickers. "What do you mean?"

"You opened her locker, and you took everything out of it. Why?"

"I don't know what you're talking about."

Boy, how did I not see through her before? She wasn't even a convincing liar.

"I saw you," I said.

"That's impossible."

"On the surveillance camera. I saw you open Ashley's locker and clear it out."

Her eyes shot to the right, then to the left. "I have to go to class."

Rachel started away from me. Working more on instinct than reason, I reached out and grabbed her arm, holding her in place.

"Why did you lie to me?"

"Let go of me."

"Where's Ashley?"

"Mickey, you're hurting me!"

I let go then. She pulled her arm back and rubbed where I'd grabbed near the elbow. People walked past us, whispering.

"I'm sorry," I said to her.

"I have to get to class."

She started to walk away.

"I'm not going to let this go, Rachel."

She stopped and looked at me again. "I can explain."

"I'm listening."

"Meet me after school. Alone. No Ema or Spoon. I'll tell you everything."

And then she was off again.

chapter 18

THE REST OF THE SCHOOL DAY went by slowly. I kept staring at the clock, but it felt as though the minute hand were bathed in syrup. I tried to figure out how Rachel could be involved, but nothing came to me. Then I reminded myself that it was pointless to speculate, that in just a few more hours I would know.

There were only five minutes left before the end of school—five minutes until I could get back to Rachel and hear her explanation—when the intercom in Mr. Berlin's physics class beeped. He picked it up, listened, and then said, "Mickey Bolitar? Please report to Mr. Grady's office."

The class gave me a collective "ooo."

I hadn't met Mr. Grady yet, but I knew who he was. First and foremost in my mind, Mr. Grady was the school's varsity basketball coach. He was a man I hoped to soon know quite well. But the reason for the class's "ooo" had to do with his real job: vice principal in charge of discipline—in short, the school's disciplinarian.

I collected my things and started for the front office. I wasn't nervous. My firm belief, immodest as this might sound, was that Mr. Grady wanted to welcome me to the school. Yes, I had worked hard to keep my game under wraps, but what with my height, my pedigree as Myron's nephew, and the way the guys down at the pickup games in Newark gossiped, it would be surprising if Mr. Grady hadn't at least heard about me.

That, I hoped, was the reason for calling me down to his office.

Or was it?

Had I done anything wrong? I didn't think so. I thought about grabbing Rachel in the hallway. Suppose someone had seen that. Nah, that couldn't be it. What would a witness do? Go to Grady's office and tell him? And then what? He'd contact Rachel and she would tell him it was nothing.

Or would she?

I got to his office and knocked on the door.

"Come in."

I opened the door. Mr. Grady sat at his desk and peered at me over his reading glasses. His suit jacket was off. He wore a short-sleeve dress shirt that probably fit a few years ago, but now it worked like a tourniquet around his neck and torso. He stood and hoisted his belt up. His pants were olive green. His hair was heavily thinning, pulled back and plastered to his scalp.

"Mickey Bolitar?"

"Yes."

"Sit down, son."

I glanced at the clock behind him. I really didn't have time for this now. School let out in two minutes—two minutes until I confronted Rachel again. He saw my hesitation and said, "Sit down," with a little more authority. I sat.

"Do you play ball?" he asked.

Ah. So I was right. "Yes."

"Your uncle was some player."

"Yes, so I've heard."

Grady nodded. He put his hands on his stomach. I wanted to move this along but I wasn't sure what to say.

"When are tryouts?" I asked, just to say something.

"In two weeks," he said. "The varsity—that's for my juniors and seniors—will be on Monday. The JV—that's for the sophomores and freshmen—will be on Tuesday." He met my eye and said, "I don't believe in playing sophomores on varsity, except in very rare instances. In fact, in the twelve years I've been coaching here, I haven't had a sophomore on varsity yet, and with so many returning starters . . ."

He didn't finish the thought. He didn't need to. I had

215

learned a long time ago that you shouldn't talk about your game—your game should do the talking for you. So I nodded and said nothing.

The final bell rang. I started to stand, figuring we were done, when Mr. Grady said, "But that's not why I called you down here. I mean, this isn't about basketball."

He waited for me to respond, so I said, "Oh?"

"I received a report that you got into a physical altercation with another student." I must have looked confused. "Troy Taylor. In the school parking lot."

Oh boy. I debated going with the he-started-it defense, but beginning a relationship with a new basketball coach by going after his captain seemed an unwise move. I went with silence.

"Do you want to tell me about it?"

"It was nothing," I said. "A misunderstanding. We moved past it."

"I see." He sat back down and fiddled with his pen. "I don't know where you went to school before here, Mickey, but at this school, we have a strict no-fighting rule. If you lay a hand on another student, it's automatic suspension with a possibility for expulsion. Do I make myself clear?"

"Yes, sir."

I couldn't help it. My eyes glanced at the clock. Grady saw it.

"Someplace to go, son?"

"I'm supposed to meet a friend after school."

"That's not going to happen today."

"Excuse me?"

"I'm letting you off easy with this one. Detention. Today."

"It can't be today," I said.

"Why not?"

"I have a really important meeting after school."

"You're currently staying with your uncle, correct?"

"Yes."

Mr. Grady picked up the phone on his desk. The phone was big and heavy and looked like something you'd see in a black-and-white movie on cable. "Maybe you can give me his phone number. I can call and explain why you'll be late. If he says it's an emergency and you can't serve it today, fine, you can serve detention tomorrow."

Panic made my mouth start flapping: "Troy took my friend's laptop. He grabbed me first. I just defended myself."

Grady cocked an eyebrow. "That really the way you want to play this, son?"

No. I calmed myself. There was really no option here. I asked whether it was okay for me to send a quick text before serving detention. Grady said that it was. I texted Rachel that I'd be out in an hour and could she please wait for me?

No reply came in.

I had never done detention before, but then again I'd never spent time in an American high school. I wasn't sure what to expect, but it was basically one hour of pure boredom. You sit in the driver's ed classroom with other students.

No phone, no gadgets, no books, nothing. Most kids put their heads on the desk and took naps. I looked for patterns in the tile floor. Then I started reading all the posted safety information on drinking and driving, texting and driving, speeding, and whatever else could happen.

I thought about my dad. I thought about our car crash and wondered if the driver of the SUV was drunk or texting or speeding. I thought about the paramedic with the sandy hair and the green eyes and how his face told me that my life would never be the same.

When the hour was finally over—the slowest hour imaginable—I grabbed my cell phone and checked for texts.

Nothing from Rachel.

Feeling dejected, I headed out the front door of the school—and there she was. I rushed over to her. "Thanks for waiting."

Rachel nodded, said nothing. She looked distracted, unsure of herself.

"So you were going to explain?" I asked.

"You said you saw me on a surveillance video, right?"

Now I could see. She wasn't distracted. She was frightened. "That's right."

"How? I mean, how did you get a hold of school security stuff?"

I shook my head. I didn't trust her enough to tell her about Spoon. "It's not important."

"It is to me," she said. "Do other people know?"

"What's the difference?"

"Why would you have been looking at video surveillance?"

"I told you. I'm trying to figure out what happened to Ashley. Why were you at her locker?"

"Why do you think?"

"I don't have a clue," I said. "You told me you didn't really know her."

"I didn't," she said.

I spread my hands. "Yet there you are, cleaning out her locker."

Rachel looked off and shook her head. "You don't get it."

"You're right. I don't. So explain it to me. And while you're at it, why don't you explain to me why you were pretending to be my friend?"

"Ashley asked me to do that."

"Ashley asked you to pretend to be my friend?"

Rachel sighed, as though there were no way I would understand. "She wanted me to check up on you. She wanted to make sure that you were okay."

"Okay?" My head was spinning. "What are you talking about?"

"Ashley didn't want you hurt. She didn't want you involved."

"Involved in what?"

"It's not my place to say. She said I shouldn't tell you."

My heart picked up speed. "Wait, hold up. Ashley said that?"

"Yes."

"So you know where she is?"

She didn't reply.

"Rachel?"

She looked up at me slowly. Our eyes met. I know that I should know better by now, but if this was an act, if I was just being played . . . No. They say the eyes don't lie. I saw something there, in the way she looked at me, and it wasn't just deception. "Yes," Rachel finally said. "I know where Ashley is."

"Where?"

"Come on," Rachel said, finally breaking eye contact. "I'll show you."

chapter 19

WE WALKED IN COMFORTABLE SILENCE for a while. I
tried to wait her out, hoping that she would volunteer some
information, but she didn't. Finally I asked, "Where are we
going?"

"My house."

"And Ashley is there?"

She made a face like maybe-yes, maybe-no. "You'll see."

"What does that mean? What happened?"

"I'll let Ashley explain."

"I'd rather hear it from you."

"Like I said before, it's not my place to explain."

We walked in silence a little more.

"Mickey?"

I looked at her.

"I wasn't pretending to be your friend. I mean, Ashley did ask me to look after you and maybe that's why I started talking to you at first, but then . . ." She stopped, keeping her eyes on the pavement, and said, "Never mind."

I wanted to do something here, reach out and take her hand, something. But I didn't know what. My cell phone buzzed. It was a text from Ema: **where r u?**

I showed it to Rachel. She shook her head. "Don't answer it."

I nodded, put my phone away. Rachel's sprawling estate—it wasn't a house, it was an estate—sat atop a hill. There was an electric gate at the end of the driveway. Rachel pressed a code into the number pad and it swung open. We started up the drive.

"Are your parents home?" I asked.

A smile crossed her lips. "No."

The smile was saying something, but I wasn't sure what.

"Is Ashley here?"

"Yes."

"Where?"

"The guesthouse in the back."

"How long has she been here?"

"Over a week."

"So your parents know?"

"Let's just say"—again she flashed the small smile, only this time I could see it was a sad one—"that my parents aren't around very much."

Everything about this place said big bucks. We walked around back, past the marble patio and clay tennis court. There was a small house next to the pool. I gestured toward it with my chin.

"Ashley's in there?" I said.

"Yes."

I swallowed and hurried my step. This was it. All my questions were about to be answered. We got to the door. Rachel had a key in her hand. She put it in the lock and turned the knob.

"Ashley?" she said.

There was no reply.

"Ashley?"

Still nothing. We stepped all the way in. The bed was made. The room was neat. But no one was there. I looked at Rachel. Her face was pale now, her eyes wide. I glanced around the room, and there, on the table next to the bed, was a note. I picked it up. Rachel was next to me, looking over my shoulder.

RACHEL–
    SORRY TO JUST RUN OFF LIKE THIS. CAN'T EXPLAIN WITHOUT DRAWING YOU INTO THIS DEEPER. THANK YOU FOR HIDING ME, BUT I CAN'T CAN'T HIDE FOREVER. DON'T CALL THE POLICE. THIS IS SOMETHING I HAVE TO DO.

                                        –ASHLEY

"I don't understand," Rachel said. "She was terrified."

We were inside Rachel's house now. We had quickly checked just to make sure that Ashley wasn't here. She wasn't. No one was. The big house was as silent as a mausoleum.

"Tell me what happened," I said.

"A little more than a week ago, we had tryouts for the cheerleading squad. There was only room for three new girls this year, and maybe fifty girls showed up. One of them was Ashley."

That surprised me. "She was trying out for cheerleading?"

Rachel nodded.

"So how did it go?"

"Not well. The new girls were being selected by three of us. Cathy, Brittany, and me. I thought that she was good, had real talent, but her audition was, well, it was weird."

"In what way?"

"This place is old-school. We do classic cheerleading. It's more gymnastic based. Most of the girls did familiar routines—acrobatics, tumbling, showing that they could help form a pyramid. That kind of thing. Ashley, on the other hand, danced. I thought she was pretty good, showed a lot of promise, but the other girls thought . . ."

"Thought what?"

"That her routine was a tad"—she stopped, either searching for the word or afraid to say it—"well, it was pretty racy. Not over the top. But it was enough to get the other girls going."

224

I said nothing. I thought about the Plan B Go-Go Lounge and wanted to close my eyes.

"And so Ashley finishes this, and then, well, she's waiting for applause. No one claps. Ashley is standing there, all nervous, waiting for feedback. And the girls just dig into her. First Cathy snickers and says, 'Where's your stripper pole?' Then they start in on her clothes, her hair, the whole thing."

"What's wrong with her clothes and hair?"

"You're a guy, so you wouldn't notice. The clothes are secondhand."

I couldn't believe what I was hearing. "So what? You guys made fun of her for having old clothes? Are you really that snobby?"

Rachel looked hurt when I said that. "You guys?"

"I just meant—"

"I'm not a snob. I don't care how much money someone has. That's not the point."

"What is then?"

"The clothes weren't even secondhand, so much as third- or fourth-hand. There was a pretense here. It's like she went to a thrift shop and searched for Eighties Prep. I mean, a monogrammed sweater?"

"I still don't get it."

"It was like," Rachel said, "she was trying to look like something she wasn't. Like she was in disguise. Anyway, it got cruel. Everyone started laughing at her."

"Did you laugh at her too?"

225

"No," she said quickly. Then Rachel looked down at the floor and her voice got softer. "But I didn't stop it either. I should have. I mean, she was just standing there, alone, in front of everybody. She didn't know us. She looked so vulnerable and there we were, laughing in her face, until finally, she just ran off."

Rachel stopped then. I tried to imagine the scene, how it must have wounded Ashley to hear those laughs.

"Nice," I said, trying to sound sarcastic without crossing into bitter.

"Yeah, I know."

"So what happened next?"

"I ran after her. You know, to apologize. She started down Collins Drive, so I headed that way. I looked down Mountainside Road, and there, about a hundred yards down, I spotted her walking toward Northfield Avenue. I called out, but Ashley didn't stop. I don't know if she didn't hear me or was just ignoring me." She stopped and swallowed. "And then something weird happened."

"What?"

"A car screeched up to her, and this big guy jumped out of the passenger side before the car had even stopped. Ashley started to back up, but he was on her fast. I mean, it was a second, maybe two. He picked her up and threw her over his shoulder. She screamed. I screamed too. I ran as fast as I could toward them. I didn't even think, you know? I just started running and screaming. The big guy ignored me. He started to throw her in the back, but Ashley resisted. She got her hands on the outside of the door, trying to pull herself back. The big guy started pushing, but she held on. The driver yelled, 'Hurry!' and then the big guy actually made a fist. He reared back to hit her, but I was closer now. I screamed again, kept trying to get his attention. I took out my cell phone and pointed it at him. I shouted, 'I called nine-one-one and I'm recording everything. Let her go.'"

"Were you?" I asked.

"Was I what?"

"Recording it."

"I wish. You have to find the app button and click it and then hit Record . . . There was no time. I was just reacting."

My cell phone buzzed again. I took a quick glance. It was from Ema again: **where r u??! IMPORTANT.**

No time to respond now. I nodded at Rachel to continue.

"Anyway, the big man finally turned toward me. Ashley used that. She kicked out, and the guy stumbled back. She broke free and ran. The guy was going to go after her, but he saw me with the phone and I guess he decided to cut his losses. He jumped back in the car. Before they peeled out, the driver called out in the spookiest voice, 'You can't hide forever, Ash, you know I'll find you.' And then they were gone."

"Did you get the license plate number?"

Rachel nodded. "I memorized it and then I ran over to

make sure Ashley was okay. I started to dial nine-one-one for real now when Ashley put her hand on mine and whispered, 'You can't call the cops.' She sounded so scared."

Rachel had her hands in her lap. She started nervously twirling a ring on her right index finger. My phone buzzed again. Then another time. I didn't even look.

"Why didn't she want you to call the police?"

"She said it would make it worse. She begged me not to, so, I mean, what was I going to do? We went back here, to my house. At first, Ashley didn't want to talk about it. She just kept crying and blaming herself. I told her it wasn't her fault, but she wouldn't listen. I got on the computer and Googled the Kents' phone number. I said, 'Let's call your parents,' but again she stopped me. She told me that her real last name wasn't Kent. What she did was, she found a Kasselton resident without any kids in the school system. Then she just pretended to be their child so she could enroll in the school."

"You can just do that?"

Rachel shrugged. "I guess."

"So the Kents didn't know about her?"

"I don't think so. She said she worked at a horrible nightclub and that everyone there thought that some creepy guy kidnapped her and sold her overseas into white slavery. But really she escaped."

White slavery, I thought, feeling a chill slip down my spine. Candy had talked about Antoine making girls disappear into "White Death." White death, white slavery—they had to be the same thing.

"So," Rachel said, "here she was, in Kasselton, hiding from her past until she got sent to the final place."

"The final place?"

"That was what she said. Like staying here in Kasselton was only temporary. But she liked being here. She said . . . she said she'd never been this happy before. She wanted to find a way to make Kasselton her final place, but they found her. That, she said, was her mistake."

Another buzz. I risked a quick look. Yep, it was Ema:

I need to show you something. promise me you won't get mad.

"The guy in the car," I said to Rachel. "Did he have a tattoo on his face?"

"No. He was tall—your height maybe—but twice your size. And he was black."

I thought about Derrick the bouncer at the Plan B Go-Go Lounge. "How did they find her?"

"Ashley didn't know, but I think I figured it out," Rachel said.

"How?"

"Both of you were new students, right?"

"Right."

"So you participated in Ms. Owens's weird bonding orientation."

I remembered. Man, how dumb had that been? "So?"

"We get the *Star-Ledger* delivered every day. They did a story on it. One of the pictures was some kind of relay race. And there, pretty clear to see, was Ashley."

The *Star-Ledger* was the state's biggest newspaper and it covered Newark. It made sense.

"Okay," I said, "so you're back here at your house. What did you guys do next?"

"Ashley needed to hide and figure that out. I told her she could stay here with me." She saw me opening my mouth, so she held up her hand to stop me. "To answer your next question, my parents are divorced. My mother lives in Florida. My father is on his third trophy wife. They travel a lot."

"Do you have any brothers or sisters?"

"One older brother. He's in college. We do have full-time help, but they only go into the pool house on Thursdays."

"So you put her up out there?"

"Yes. Ashley worried that the guys who tried to grab her would keep searching. She said they'd be relentless—that they might go after her only friend here."

"That," I said, "would be me."

She nodded. "I went into her locker to get out her notebook and clothes. She'd written your name and number down there. You'd shared notes. If those guys found them, they'd know that you two were close. But even then, she still wasn't positive that they hadn't approached you."

"So that's why she asked you to keep an eye on me."

"Yes."

"Which you did. You even got me to be your history partner."

Rachel glanced around the ridiculously formal living room as though she had never seen it before. It looked like something out of a European palace. We sat on a couch with very little padding.

"Why?" I asked.

"Why what?"

"You barely knew Ashley. She wasn't your friend."

"True."

"And it was dangerous. They'd seen your face. They could have tracked you down."

"I guess."

"So why did you help her?"

Rachel thought about it a minute. "Because she was in trouble. Because I didn't help her at the cheerleading audition. I don't know. I wanted to help. It just felt like the right thing to do. I don't want to make it sound like more than it is, but I get that way. I felt somehow obligated."

I said nothing. I knew what she meant. My father and mother lived lives of obligation. If you asked them why, they would have given an answer like Rachel's.

The phone buzzed again. I sighed and grabbed it. No surprise—it was yet another message from Ema: **wanted to show you in person but will send image now. it's been here for months.**

There was a photographic attachment. I clicked on it and the photograph came up. For a moment, I couldn't figure out what it was. It was a close-up of some sort, and blurry. I saw skin. I turned my head a little, focused my eyes, and then I felt my blood run cold.

It was a blue-and-green tattoo. I could see that now. And it was a tattoo of that same emblem—the blurry butterfly with the animal-eye wings.

With shaking hands, I typed: **Whose tattoo is that??**

There was a delay. Rachel looked over at me. I waited for the next text. It took longer than it should. Finally, a full minute later, almost as though the very letters were hesitating, came Ema's response: **it's mine.**

chapter 20

WITH MY FAKE DRIVER'S LICENSE in my wallet, I picked up Ema on the outskirts of Kasselton Avenue. She slid into the Ford Taurus with a sheepish look on her face.

"I don't understand any of this," I said.

"It was Agent's idea," Ema explained, talking fast.

That was where we were headed—to Tattoos While U Wait to confront Agent.

"Over the summer, I went to Agent for a back tattoo. I wanted something big and dramatic. So he drew up this elaborate artwork, with swirls and lettering and then . . ." She stopped. "You're looking at me funny."

"You're kidding, right?"

She said nothing.

"Of course I'm looking at you funny," I said, with more

snap in my voice than I intended. "That tattoo was in an old photograph in Bat Lady's house. It was on that tombstone in her backyard. And someone even drew it on a placard marking my father's grave. Now all of a sudden it's a tattoo on your back?"

"I know. I don't understand it either. See, the tattoo is pretty big and the butterfly is just a small part. It wasn't even in the original plan, but Agent said he was inspired."

I shook my head. "So why didn't you tell me about it as soon as you saw it on that tombstone?"

"You ran off, remember? You got arrested."

"And what about yesterday? At Baumgart's? Or today at school?"

Ema said nothing.

"Hello?"

"Stop yelling at me," she said.

"I'm not yelling. It's just . . . how could you keep that from me?"

"Well, why didn't you tell me you were secretly meeting with Miss Hot-Bod today? Huh?" She folded her arms. "You don't tell me everything. I don't tell you everything."

"Ema?"

"What?"

"That's a load of crap and you know it. Why didn't you tell me about the tattoo?"

Ema looked out the front windshield. We were getting

closer to Agent's place. I let it sit. There was no reason to push, not yet, but I wanted to know what was going on. I switched on the radio, but Ema reached for the knob and turned it off.

She sat back and said, "I was afraid, okay?"

"Afraid of what?"

Ema shook her head and frowned. She wore a silver ring on every finger, giving her a kind of gypsy vibe. "For a bright guy, you can be so dense."

"Yep. So why don't you explain it to me?"

"At first, I wasn't even sure. Like maybe that thing on the tombstone just looked like my tattoo, but it wasn't the same."

"At first," I repeated.

"Right."

"And then?"

I took a quick glance at her. A tear ran down her cheek. "Do I look like I have a lot of friends to you?"

I said nothing.

Ema's voice was barely a whisper. "I thought maybe you'd get angry. Or blame me. Or not believe or trust me. I thought"—she turned away now so I couldn't see her face—"that you wouldn't want to be my friend anymore."

The hurt in her voice broke my heart. When we came to the next stoplight, I said, "Ema?"

"What?"

"Look at me."

She did. Her eyes were moist.

"I trust you with my life," I said. "And like it or not, you're the best friend I've ever had."

There was nothing more to say after that. We drove the rest of the way to the tattoo parlor in silence.

Tattoos While U Wait was in full swing when we arrived. We hurried to Agent's chair in the back, but no one was there. I stood at the empty chair as if I could make Agent materialize with just a stare. Nothing happened.

Ema said, "Mickey?"

I looked over at her. She was pointing at a mirror on Agent's desk. We both moved toward it. We stood there, afraid to move. There, taped to the lower left-hand corner of the mirror, was that same butterfly emblem.

"Hey, Ema. You two like?"

I spun toward the voice. No, it wasn't Agent. This guy was, I assumed, either another tattoo artist or a frequent client. Every sliver of visible skin had ink on it. I thought about tattoos, about the connection, about the tattoo on Ema's back, the tattoo on Antoine's face—and most horrifically, the Auschwitz concentration camp tattoo forced upon a young girl named Elizabeth Sobek.

"Hey, Ian," Ema said, trying to sound nonchalant. "Do you know where Agent is?"

"He's not here." Ian looked at Ema. Then he looked at me.

I gave him flat eyes and said, "Uh, yeah, we can see that."

"Do you know where he is?" Ema asked. "Or when he'll be back?"

"He took off," Ian said. "He won't be back for a while."

"What's a while?" I asked. "Like tonight or . . ."

"Not tonight. Not this week." Now Ian faced me full on, studying me as though I were a horse he was considering purchasing. "You must be Mickey."

That surprised me. "Do I know you?" I said.

"Nah. Agent told me you'd come by."

I glanced at Ema. She shrugged to show that she didn't get it either. "He did?"

Ian nodded. "He asked me to do the work on you, but he didn't say where. Arm, thigh, back . . . where do you want it?"

I took a step closer to him. "We didn't make an appointment."

"Oh, I know."

"So when you say you expected us to come by—"

"Agent didn't say when. He just said you would. Stop by, that is. And he said that when you do, I should take care of you. Look, he left the artwork right there for you."

He pointed with his chin at the lower left-hand corner of the mirror—at the same image I had seen in Bat Lady's house, by my father's grave, and on Ema.

"Do you like it?" Ian asked.

It took me a moment or two to find my voice. "What is it?" I asked, my voice sounding oddly hushed in my own ear.

Now it was Ian who looked surprised. "You don't know?"

I shook my head.

"Agent didn't tell you?"

"No."

Ian shook his head. "Man, that's odd. Why would he think you'd want that tattoo if you don't know what it is?"

"I don't know," I said. "But could you tell me what it is?"

Ian mulled that over for a moment. We waited. Finally he said, "That's a butterfly."

I stifled my sign of impatience. "Yeah, we can see that."

"More specifically," he went on, "that's the Swordgrass Brown Tisiphone Abeona."

I felt my stomach drop at that last word. I swallowed hard, repeating his words in my own head. "What did you say?"

Something in my voice must have come out as a threat. Ian put his hands up as though warding me off. "Whoa, calm down, dude."

I took a deep breath. "What did you call that butterfly?"

"Hey, Agent told me that. He talked about it all the time."

"Please just"—I tried to keep my voice in check—"tell me the name of the butterfly again."

"Swordgrass Brown Tisiphone Abeona."

I swallowed. "Abeona."

"Yep," Ian said, smiling now. "Hey, you know about Abeona?"

I said nothing.

"Me and Agent, we were into ancient gods and goddesses, you know, because people want them as tats. Abeona was a Roman goddess. Did you know that?"

I stood there, stunned. I thought back to my father's resignation letter: "*I know that no one really ever leaves the Abeona Shelter.* . . ."

"I'm not a big fan of this one myself," Ian continued, "but see, Abeona was a sort of shielding goddess. She protected children when they first left the safety of their parents, guarding them during their first voyage away from home. Like that. And what's weird about this butterfly, well, the name, right? Tisiphone was one of the Furies, you know, the Ancient Greek gods? She punished the big crimes—murder and stuff—especially when it came to children in danger. Do you know her story?"

I shook my head, afraid to speak.

"Okay, see Tisiphone's father, Alcmaeon, accidentally left her and her brother, Amphilochus, with Creon, who was king of Thebes. Now Tisiphone, even as a young girl, was a total hottie, so Creon's evil wife sold her into slavery. What the wife didn't realize was that the guy who bought Tisiphone was actually working for Alcmaeon, her father. See? It was all a big plan to save his children."

"How do you know all this?" I asked.

"Oh man, Agent talked about it all the time. That's why he loved this butterfly. I think it's native to Australia or New Zealand, someplace like that, but it's named after both

Tisiphone and Abeona. That's why he loved to put it in his work. See those eyes on the wings? Like they're watching you. For him, the symbol is all about rescuing children. It's all about giving them protection and shelter."

Shelter. The Abeona Shelter. Where my father worked all those years . . .

"Ian," Ema said, "do you know how we can reach Agent?"

Ian smiled. "He said you'd ask that. So he wanted me to be clear."

"Well?"

"No. There is no way to reach Agent. None." He gestured toward me. "So what do you say, Mickey? You ready to get the tattoo?"

My cell phone buzzed. I looked down and saw it was a text from Rachel: **Got a clue on Ashley.**

"Not now," I said, rushing to the door.

Maybe not ever.

chapter 21

WE WERE GOING TO MEET at Myron's house, but a quick call to his cell phone stopped that.

"Where are you?" Myron asked me.

I didn't like the tone in his voice.

"I'm with friends," I said.

"Driving what car?"

Uh-oh. Ema was studying my face. I mouthed the word "Trouble."

"I know your father taught you to drive," he said to me. "But it's illegal. You know that."

"I'm just at a friend's house," I said.

"Whose?"

"Rachel. You met her last night."

"You couldn't walk there?"

"Uh, I, look, she'd never go out with a kid. So, well, I told her I was older."

Wow, could that have sounded any lamer?

"You lied?"

"No, not really. I just let her believe . . . Look, I'll tell her the truth. Then I'll drive the car home and not use it again."

"Mickey," Myron said, putting on his parental voice, "do you know what will happen to you if Chief Taylor catches you driving?"

I said nothing.

"Just leave the car there," Myron said. "Walk home. I'll find a way to get it back here."

"Okay," I said. "Thank you. But can I stay a little while longer?"

"Only if you promise to tell her the truth," Myron said. "You shouldn't lie to her."

Oh boy.

"You're absolutely right," I said, choking on the words. I wanted to tell him to stick it, but more than that, I did *not* want him looking for me. "I'm so sorry. I'll tell her right away. Bye."

When I hung up, Ema started laughing.

"What?" I said.

"Your uncle bought that?"

I couldn't help but smile. "He's new to this."

"I guess so."

We called Rachel back and changed the meeting spot to her house. The gate guarding the driveway opened the moment I turned into it. Rachel must have been watching. Ema sat in silence. She didn't comment at all as we drove up to the mansion.

"I still don't know where you live," I said to Ema.

"We got bigger worries, don't you think?"

She had a point. When we pulled up to the house, Rachel was already standing in the doorway. Ema stared at her with an expression on her face I would have to call resigned.

"What's wrong?" I asked.

"She is beautiful, isn't she?"

I didn't know how to reply to that, so I didn't. I pulled the door handle and stepped out. Rachel smiled when she saw me. The smile dimmed a bit when she saw Ema. We both headed up the walk toward her. Rachel watched Ema. Ema watched Rachel. I didn't know what to do.

Rachel said, "Ashley didn't want anyone to know about this."

"It's okay," I said. "Ema's been in on this from the beginning."

Rachel didn't look happy about my answer. Neither did Ema. I tried to move us forward.

"You said you had a clue about Ashley?"

Rachel looked wary.

"It's okay," I said.

She sighed and led us into the house. We sat in the same opulent room where Rachel and I had been just a few short hours ago. "This laptop was in the pool house. Ashley used it to check her e-mail. I was able to get into her account."

"How?" I asked.

Rachel looked uncomfortable. "My father is rarely around," she said, "but that doesn't mean he doesn't like to keep an eye on me. Last year, he put this parental spy software on all the home computers so he could monitor what I was doing."

Ema said, "Yuck."

"I know, right?"

Ema shook her head and said, "Parents."

I could see a softening between the two. It wasn't much. *Softening* might be too strong a word. *Thawing* might be more accurate. But it was there.

"But the thing is, my dad is pretty bad with computers. He just bought some package online—he really doesn't know what he's doing. So I figured out what was going on and then I found his codes, and, well, now he sees what I want him to see, if you catch my drift. Not that I have anything to hide anyway. That's the thing. I don't, but—okay, never mind." Rachel tucked her hair behind her ear. "Anyway, the point is, even though Ashley deleted her history, I was able to see what she'd done on the computer."

"And?" I said.

"She got this e-mail earlier today."

Rachel handed me a printout. It was short and sweet:

Ash—

   I'm in big trouble. He thinks I hid you. You know how
he gets. You know what he can do. Please, Ash. Please
come back and help me.

And then, on the bottom, I saw who had sent the e-mail:

Candy

"So," Rachel said, "the question is, who is Candy?"

"I know," I said, feeling the fear return. I didn't see any other option. I had wanted more than anything to stay away from that awful place, and yet somehow I knew that it would end there. Even if it meant going up against Buddy Ray and his big bodyguard again. Even if it meant going up against Antoine LeMaire. Even if it meant facing the White Death.

I could see Bat Lady, who was somehow connected with my father, somehow connected with the Abeona Shelter, mouthing the words to me: *Save Ashley.*

My father had spent his life working for the Abeona Shelter. Now maybe I understood what his real job was. I didn't believe in fate or destiny. I didn't even believe in a calling or a purpose. How had Rachel put it?

"*It just felt like the right thing to do.*"

It was that simple and yet that deep. It was an obligation. Even if I wanted to turn away, I couldn't.

I had to save Ashley.

chapter 22

RACHEL AND EMA had been in the same schools for nearly a decade and had never spoken. One was the beautiful cheerleader. The other was the picked-on outcast. And I, Mickey Bolitar, had finally found a way to unite them.

How?

By saying the following: "I need to do this alone."

Rachel and Ema stood side by side, arms folded across their chests.

"Oh no," Ema said, "you're not leaving us behind."

"We're going too," Rachel said.

"And don't tell us it isn't safe," Ema added.

Rachel: "If it's not safe for us, it's not safe for you."

Ema: "Right, so don't give us your sexist nonsense."

Rachel: "Exactly. We aren't girls who need protecting from a big, strong man."

There may have been more—I confess that I started tuning them out—but I had no chance anyway. Surrender, I could see, was inevitable, so why delay it?

"So what's the plan?" Ema asked.

I checked my watch. It was nine P.M. "I don't know. I guess we head down to the Plan B Go-Go Lounge and see if we can find Candy or Ashley."

Rachel said, "They'll recognize you."

She had a point. "Okay, let's brainstorm a little and see what we come up with."

My cell phone rang again. I looked down and saw it was Uncle Myron. I answered with a tentative "Hello?"

"It's getting late," Myron said. "Did you tell Rachel the truth?"

"Yes."

"You sure?"

"She's sitting right here. Do you want me to hand her the phone?"

"No need. I found her address online. My partner Esperanza is with me. We're on our way to pick you up and get the car."

My eyes widened. Ema and Rachel saw it and moved closer. I tilted the phone so they could hear. "Not now," I said. "We're doing our history project."

"You two are in the same history class?" Myron asked.

"Yes."

"So that would make you both sophomores," Myron said, and I thought I heard a little something smug in his voice. "Rachel would know that. Why would she think a sophomore was old enough to drive?"

He was on to me.

"Hold on a second, Myron, I got another call coming in." I put him on hold and started for the door.

"What gives?" Rachel said.

"Hurry, he'll be here soon, and he'll take away the car. We need to go now."

We all sprinted for the Ford Taurus. I got in the driver's seat. Rachel and Ema both hesitated, not sure where to sit, but Rachel quickly broke that deadlock. She opened the front passenger door and said, "You sit here, Ema."

Ema did as she was told. Rachel closed the door and hopped into the back.

I pulled out of the long drive and headed to the left. By now Myron had hung up and tried to call me several more times. I didn't pick it up. Rachel looked behind her and said, "Does your uncle drive a Ford Taurus too?"

"Yes."

"Uh-oh, he's pulling up to the gate."

I stepped on the gas pedal, made a quick left, then a right, working my way through the town streets until I was sure that we weren't being followed. Then I took the main artery down to Newark.

Twenty minutes later—after a long debate with Rachel

and Ema that I clearly lost—I found a parking space across the street and down the block from the Plan B Go-Go Lounge. From here, I had a pretty good view of the front door, but that didn't appease me.

"I don't like this," I said.

"It's the only way," Rachel said. "You know that."

"We'll be fine," Ema added.

I shook my head. Rachel and Ema had hammered home the obvious: I couldn't go into the club again. They had seen my face. I had even injured Derrick the bouncer, who, thank goodness, was not currently working the door. Rachel had come up with a simple plan: she and Ema would go in, pretending to be looking for work. That would give them a chance to get inside and look around and hopefully spot either Ashley or, based on my description, Candy.

"I could wear a disguise," I said. "I could get in that way."

Rachel and Ema snickered at that.

"Like what?" Rachel asked. "A fake mustache? A blond wig? And suppose they ask for ID and see your old face?"

I had no reply.

"We've been over this," Ema added.

"I still don't like it."

"Tough," Rachel said. "Look, Ema will have her cell phone on the whole time." She used a much better carrier than I did—I currently had one bar, she had five. "You'll be able to hear everything. It's a public place—what are they going to do? We also have a code word, right?"

"Yellow," I said.

"Exactly. We'll say 'yellow' if we feel like we are in over our heads."

"We should think about this," I said.

"We did," Ema said—and before I could argue anymore, Rachel and Ema were out on the street walking toward that club. My cell phone rang. I had already blocked out Myron, so I knew that it wasn't him. I looked down and saw that it was Ema. I picked it up and said, "Hello?"

"Can you hear me okay?" Ema asked.

"Yes."

"Put your phone on mute so they won't hear anything from your end," Ema said.

I did. I watched them head up to the front door. Rachel wore fitted jeans. Ema was, as always, decked out in full black armor. I knew that Rachel would have no trouble getting in. She would, I was sure, be welcomed. My bigger fear was that she'd be *too* welcomed. Ema had pointed out that she might have more trouble convincing the bouncers that she was applying for work as a dancer, to which Rachel frowned and said, "Nonsense, you look hot."

With anyone else it would have sounded phony and patronizing. With Rachel, well, even Ema bought it.

I focused my eyes on the two bouncers at the front door. They were both far smaller than my friend from yesterday, the one who had tried to grab Ashley off the street, the one who had my arms pinned until I head-butted him. I wondered

251

whether I had broken his nose, but I wasn't about to lose too much sleep over it.

The bouncers spotted Rachel and Ema walking toward the door. I don't think too many women came here as patrons, especially on their own. Rachel and Ema both stopped in front of the door. I could hear the conversation through my cell phone.

The bouncer on the right said, "Hello, ladies, is there something I can do for you?"

"We would like to see someone about work," Rachel said.

"What kind of work?"

"Dancing, waitressing, whatever."

The bouncer on the left said, "The boss will love you. But her"—he pointed at Ema—"I mean, no way."

I wanted to punch that guy in the face.

The bouncer on the right slapped the other bouncer's arm. "Dude, that's just rude."

"Huh?"

"Yeah," Rachel said, "that's rude."

"I think she's pretty," Right Bouncer said, smiling at Ema. "You got a sweet face, sugar."

"Thank you," Ema said.

"And I bet you know how to shake it on the dance floor, am I right?"

"As rain," Ema said as they both started to enter the club. "When I get my booty shaking, worlds collide."

Back in the car, I was just smiling, thinking, *God, I love that girl*, when the driver's side window shattered. Shards of glass rained down on me. I barely had time to react when two hands reached in, grabbed me by the collar, and pulled me through the window headfirst. Remnants of the window scraped my sides, ripping my clothes and digging into my skin.

It was Derrick the bouncer. He had white tape across his nose. He looked very angry. "Well, well, well. Look who's come back to say hello."

He flung me across the street. My head crashed into the side of a car, causing a dent. I tried to regroup, but dizziness overwhelmed me. I needed a second to catch my breath, but I wasn't getting one.

Derrick kicked me in the face.

I tried to roll away, but he was on me now. A punch in the jaw made my teeth rattle. There was a knee to the ribs and then another blow, I don't even know from where, struck me in the back of the head, jarring my brain. My eyes started rolling back as the next punch landed. And then there was blackness.

When I woke up, I was being dragged through an alley by Derrick. He had one hand on the scruff of my collar. The other was holding a cell phone.

Pain flooded in, making my eyes well up with tears. My first thoughts were about Rachel and Ema. They had no backup now. Did they know that? I doubted it. If they had seen Derrick attack me, they would have screamed or done something. No, they had gone inside the club. Alone. Without anyone on the other end of the phone.

Derrick spoke into his cell phone. "Bringing him in, Buddy Ray," he said.

"Nah, no reason for that." I could hear Buddy Ray's soft voice through the phone. "We have Ash back."

"So what should I do with him?"

"Where are you?"

"Back alley."

"Any witnesses?"

Derrick said, "Nope."

"Then take care of him there," Buddy Ray said.

Take care of him?

Fear can be like a splash of cold water in the face. I debated what my next move would be. I could pretend that I was still out for a few more seconds, surprise attack him. Derrick suddenly stopped moving. He dropped me like I was a bag of laundry. I kept my eyes closed, playing possum.

"Open your eyes, kid."

When I didn't, Derrick kicked me hard in the ribs with the toe of his boot. A bolt of agony surged across my chest. My eyes flew open now. I looked up, and I was staring into the barrel of a gun.

No choice.

I dived for the gun, but Derrick was ready. Using all his weight and leverage, he hit me with a powerful side kick flush in the center of the chest. My heart stopped. That was what it felt like, like all my internal organs—heart, lungs, whatever—had shut down. I collapsed back to the ground, unable to move. Another kick to the back of my head closed my eyes. Bright lights swirled in front of my eyes. I didn't move. I don't even think I breathed. I just lay there, helpless, swimming toward unconsciousness.

Until I heard the gunshot.

chapter 23

SO THIS WAS DEATH.

I longed for my parents. I remembered a night two years ago when we were stationed with the Al-Hajaya tribe of Bedouins in the harsh desert of Jordan. We slept in goat-hair tents that protected us from the harsh conditions in the vast wasteland. I stirred slowly one morning, hearing the braying of nearby animals, my eyes blinking open to see my parents staring down at me. Mom and Dad stood together, both sporting dorky parental smiles—you know the ones, all dewy-eyed and goofy and embarrassing as a smile can be—and now I would pretty much give anything to see those dorky smiles. I'm remembering that moment so clearly now and I'm wondering—if this is indeed death—

will I see my father's dorky parental smile when I open my eyes?

But wait. If I were dead, why did I still ache from the beating Derrick gave me? My head felt as though someone had surgically implanted a jackhammer into my skull and left it running on high. Do you feel that in death? I doubted it.

I slowly opened my eyes and yes, I did indeed see a face. But it was not my father's.

It was Derrick's.

His eyes were open, unblinking, staring at nothing. A neat, perfectly circular bullet hole sat in the middle of his forehead, still leaking a little blood. There was no doubt about it. Derrick was dead.

I tried not to panic. I didn't move. I kept my head still while my eyes darted about my surroundings.

Dead Derrick and I were in the back of a van.

"Nice to see you awake, Mickey."

I looked past Derrick toward the man who spoke. The first thing I noticed about him was the tattoo on his face.

"Recognize me?" he said.

"You're Antoine LeMaire."

Something flickered on his face—doubt maybe—but then he smiled at me. "In the flesh."

I tried to fight through the pain, tried to figure my next move. Could I go for the van door behind me? Suppose it was locked. I was debating what to do when Antoine said,

"If I wanted you dead, I'd have let Derrick shoot you."

"You," I said, trying to sit up a little. "You killed him?"

"Yes."

I wasn't sure what to say. "Thank you" didn't really seem to fit. I remembered Candy's words about Antoine and this van.

"Someone told me," I said, "that once people get into this van, they're gone forever."

Antoine smiled. He had a nice smile, straight teeth and almost toothpaste-commercial white. He was either light-skinned black or darker Latino, I couldn't tell which. "Well," he said, "I guess that's mostly true." He gestured toward Derrick's dead body. "Especially in his case."

"And in mine?"

"No, Mickey. Or at least, I hope not."

"Where's Ashley?" I asked him.

"I don't know," he said. "I was looking for her too, remember?"

"So you could sell her into white slavery?"

"Ah," Antoine said, and the smile was back. "You've heard the rumors."

"Are you telling me they're not true?"

"You don't recognize me, do you, Mickey?"

"I saw you on that videotape."

"Not from that."

I hesitated. There was something familiar about him,

something distant, but the more I tried to see it, the more it stayed out of reach. "What then?"

He sighed, rolled up his shirtsleeve, and pointed to his forearm. I squinted at it, and my world, already reeling, took another major hit. I started shaking my head, lost yet again, but there it was:

The same butterfly tattoo.

"You . . . you're one of them?"

"Wouldn't 'one of us' be more accurate?"

"I don't get it."

"I think you do, Mickey."

And just like that, I realized that he was right. Without warning or even much thought, the pieces started to fall into place. The Abeona Shelter. Abeona was the goddess who protected children. From the days of Elizabeth Sobek in the 1940s, through my father's work, up until right now with Ashley, that was what they did—rescued, protected, and sheltered the young.

"Buddy Ray is the evil one," I said.

He nodded.

"He starts the girls dancing at this club," I said, "and then, well, it gets worse."

"Much worse," Antoine said. "You have no idea how depraved he can be. Ashley's mom . . . her life was not a good one. She ended up down here, dancing and more for Buddy Ray. Ashley was the only thing in her life that mattered. She protected her daughter as best she could, tried to find her a better way of life."

"But?" I said.

"But she died. Women like her . . . they don't last long. And when she died, Ashley had no one. Buddy Ray said that she owed him money. He told Ashley that she'd have to pay off the debts."

"What about Ashley's dad?"

"She never knew him. It wouldn't have mattered. Buddy Ray thinks the girls belong to him. He uses threats and violence. He holds the girls prisoner. If they don't escape, they eventually end up like Ashley's mom. But if Buddy catches them trying to run . . ."

He just left the thought in the air.

I felt my mouth go dry, but it was suddenly so clear. "So you rescue them," I said. "You pretend to kidnap girls like Ashley and sell them into white slavery. But actually, you're doing the opposite. You're trying to save them."

Antoine said nothing. He didn't have to.

"You relocate them, like you did with Ashley. First to some place close and then you move them out to someplace more permanent. But something went wrong. Ashley's picture showed up in the paper. Buddy Ray or one of his people saw it."

"That's one theory."

"You have another?" I asked.

"A teacher at your school," he said, "might work for Buddy Ray."

"Who?"

He didn't reply. I tried to put it together. "Even Ashley doesn't know your role, does she?"

"No. We grabbed her and kept her in the dark. We gave her an identity and explained what would happen next. She's responsible for herself after that."

"So when she ran scared, you didn't know where she was. You went looking for her too."

"That's right."

"You tried her locker, but that was empty. Then you beat up Dr. Kent to see what he knew."

"No, that was Buddy Ray and Derrick. They figured that since she was using that name, Kent might know something. I got there in time to save him. When his wife came home, she only spotted me. That's why she identified me to the police."

Antoine paused and studied me for a minute. "Do you feel all right, Mickey?"

I didn't know the answer. "I guess."

"Because you have work to do."

"Me?"

"I can't save Ashley. It would blow my cover. You need to do it. If you call the cops, Buddy Ray will slice her throat and make sure the body is never found. If you go to your uncle Myron—"

"Wait, how do you know my uncle?"

"I don't. But you can't go to him for help. There was a reason your father never told him about the Abeona Shelter."

I took a sharp intake of breath when he mentioned Dad. "You knew my father, didn't you?"

Antoine LeMaire took a deep breath and let it out slowly. "I knew you too. But you were very small. And you knew me as Juan."

My mouth dropped open. "My dad," I said. "He wrote you that resignation letter."

"That's right."

"He wanted out of the Abeona Shelter."

Juan's gaze flicked to the right. "Yes. For you."

For me. My father made that choice for me—and how did that work out? He died, the man I loved like no other . . . he died for me. So I could be spared any discomfort or an abnormal upbringing. For that, my father came back to the United States and died.

And what about my mother? She must have realized the truth—that her husband died because of her son. No wonder she ran away from me. No wonder she ran to a needle instead.

A pain so unbearable, a pain that made Derrick's beating seem like a light tap on the shoulder, started clawing inside me. I looked up at Juan.

"Bat Lady said that my dad's still alive," I said, my vision blurring with tears. "But he's not, is he?"

Juan's voice was almost too tender. "I don't know, Mickey."

I nodded, unable to speak.

"Do you want to help us?"

I blinked the tears away and met his eye. I wondered what my dad would want, but maybe that wasn't even important anymore.

"Yeah," I said. "Yeah, I want to help."

chapter 24

I WAS IN THE ALLEY by the same side exit where Candy had led me to safety. The cell phone was against my ear. Rachel and Ema were stalling by slowly filling out job applications, but their excuses were wearing thin.

"Oops, tee-hee," Rachel said, putting on a breathy bimbo voice. "I spelled my name wrong again. Can I get another form?"

"Sure, sweetcakes," a rough male voice said. "Why don't you use a pencil this time? So you can erase."

"Wow, what a good idea!" Rachel squealed.

"How about you?" the rough voice said.

"No, no, I'm good," Ema said. "I've been able to spell my name since I was twelve."

Another voice—this one female and older, almost matronly—said, "Okay, forget the forms. It's time for your audition."

Now I heard the men in the room snicker. I didn't like that snicker. I didn't like it at all. I reached my hand out to open the fire door.

There was no handle, nothing to grab on to. It probably just opened from the inside.

"Yeah," another guy said. "It's time to see you girls dance. You go first, Bambi."

Rachel said, "Me?"

I tried to dig into the sides of the door with my fingers, hoping to pry it open. No go.

"Enough stalling." This voice was like a gate slamming shut. "Now."

Oh man.

The older female voice said, "Calm down, Max. Bambi, it's okay. Really. But I think you should show us how you dance now."

Ema said, "Uh, it's getting kinda yellow in here."

Yellow. The code word.

I wasn't sure what to do. Sure, we had talked about a code word—but not really what to do if Rachel or Ema actually, uh, said it. I had to get them out, that much was clear, but how? If I called the cops, well, Juan/Antoine had warned me where that might lead. Do I just run through the front entrance myself? Would that work? Wouldn't that also set Buddy Ray off?

I started prying at the door again. It wouldn't give.

"Tee-hee," Rachel started up again, "okay, sure, let's do the audition. But first I have to go tinkle."

I stopped. Tinkle?

That was what one of the guys said too: "Tinkle?"

"Tee-hee. Like go to the little girls' room? Tinkle? You know, silly."

"Or as our friend Buck says," Ema added, clearly for my benefit, "we have to go wee-wee."

"Oh," a male voice said.

Then another: "The dressing room is over on the left. You might as well change into one of the, um, costumes while you're there, Bambi."

"You too, Tawny."

Tawny and Bambi. How imaginative.

I waited by the door, not sure what to do. I heard some movement and then more commotion. Hopefully they'd find a way to get alone so they could talk to me.

A few seconds later, Ema said, "Mickey?"

"Where are you?" I said.

"In the dressing room," Ema said. "Which, judging by what I'm seeing, should be called the undressing room. We haven't seen Candy yet. You still in the car?"

"No." There was no time to go into detail on my meeting

with Antoine/Juan. "I'm outside in the alley by the fire door. Ask one of the girls where it is and then let's just get out of here."

"Okay." I heard conversation. Then Ema came back on. "I think we know how to get . . ." She stopped.

"Hello?"

Nothing.

"Hello?"

Then Ema's voice came back on the line. "I think I found Candy."

"It doesn't matter," I said. "It's getting too dangerous. You two need to get out."

"Just hang tight," Ema said. "Oh, and put the mute back on."

I wanted to ask more questions, but if she wanted the mute back on, there had to be a good reason. I could hear voices again, but I couldn't really make anything out. I stood alone in the alley, hopping impatiently from one foot to the other. I tried to think of something to do, but there was really no option here.

I had to wait, no matter how helpless I felt.

Ema wasn't talking anymore. Rachel wasn't talking anymore. I could only hear background noises. I didn't know what to make of that. Suppose something happened. Suppose they couldn't talk. Was I just supposed to stand here doing nothing for . . . well, for how long? Five minutes? Ten?

An hour? I remembered Buddy Ray's face, the joy he took in hurting me. I thought about the fear in Candy's eyes when we hurried past the "dungeon."

How could I have let them go in there on their own?

Time passed. I don't know how much. It might have been ten minutes, but it was probably more like two or three. And then, just when I thought that I might jump out of my skin from worry, the fire door opened.

It was Ema.

"Get in," she said quickly.

"What? No. You get out."

She stepped aside and now I could see Rachel and Candy standing there with her.

"Get in," Ema said again.

There was no time to argue. Suddenly I was back inside that blue room with the throw pillows. The heavy fire door closed behind me. I glanced at both Ema and Rachel, who signaled that they were fine. I turned to Candy. She looked different now, though I couldn't put my finger on what exactly had changed. She looked thinner somehow, more drawn, paler. There was a quake running through her face. Her lower lip trembled.

"Where's Ashley?" I asked her.

Candy shrugged without conviction. "How would I know?"

"Because you e-mailed her," I said.

Candy looked left, then right. "Uh, I don't know what you're talking about."

But she did. No question about that now. "You e-mailed her that you were in trouble. That's why she came back here, right?"

Candy said nothing. The quake in her face got more pronounced. I put my hands on her shoulders and started shaking her. "Tell me where she is."

Candy started sobbing.

"Where is Ashley?" I demanded, my voice a little louder.

Rachel said, "Mickey . . ."

I looked at her. She shook her head. I nodded. She was right. I was being too rough. Ema moved closer, sort of pushing me away from her. Rachel took Candy in her arms and stroked her hair.

Rachel's voice was soft and comforting. "You e-mailed Ashley that you were in trouble."

Candy nodded.

"What kind of trouble?"

Candy just shook her head. "I didn't mean to hurt her."

I felt my heart lurch when she said that.

"I know," Rachel said gently. "It's okay. Just tell us what happened."

"Ashley was my best friend," Candy said.

Ema glanced at her watch, then at me. I knew what she was thinking. The "boys" would only be patient so long with Rachel's "tinkle." We had to speed this up. Ema moved to the door to keep guard.

Rachel said, "You need to tell us what happened, Candy."

Candy nodded, pulled away. She wiped away her tears with her sleeve. "We always said, Ashley and me, that we would get out of here together. You know? We had plans. We'd run away to California. We'd leave this all behind. It was just a dream. I mean, we both knew Buddy Ray would never let us go. But . . ." She looked up at Rachel, her eyes pleading. "Ashley escaped. Don't you see? I thought Antoine had gotten her. But she ran away. And she didn't take me with her."

"She left you behind," Rachel said, trying to sound understanding.

"She swore she would never do that," Candy said, crying again. "He"—now she pointed her chin at me—"he told me that Ashley was fine. That she was in some rich-kid high school. How could Ashley do that to me?"

"So you set her up," I said.

Her eyes shot hard at me. "I didn't have any choice. Buddy Ray knew I helped you. He told me if I didn't help him get her back, he'd kill me." The tears started flowing again. "How? How could Ashley have just left me like that?"

"She didn't," I said, not wanting to go into details about Antoine's real identity or the Abeona Shelter. "She was taken by surprise. If she contacted you, it would have risked everything."

"So Ashley didn't . . . ?"

"She didn't abandon you, no. Now, if you know where Ashley is . . ."

I looked at Ema. She was still checking outside the door. I turned back to Candy. Her face had fallen.

"There's no hope," Candy said.

A cold gust blew across my chest. "What happened?"

"You're just a bunch of kids. You can't defeat Buddy Ray. Do you know what he'll do if he even knows I talked to you?"

Candy quickly rolled up the sleeve of her blouse. We squinted at what she was showing us. It didn't register at first. Then Rachel gasped out loud.

There were two fresh cigarette burns on Candy's arm.

"There's more. That's all I can show you."

"Oh my God," Rachel said.

I felt my stomach do flips. "And he has Ashley? Where are they?"

Candy shook her head.

"Please tell me."

And then Candy did something that truly chilled me. She slowly lifted her head and looked all the way across the room. I followed her gaze and saw now that Candy was looking at a door.

The door that led to the dungeon.

Suddenly there were voices coming closer. Ema turned and harsh-whispered, "Mickey, hide!"

I didn't wait. I dived behind some throw pillows just as three men and one woman—the matronly one I'd heard on the phone—turned the corner and entered the room, pushing Ema aside.

"There you are, Bambi," the woman said. She had a big beehive hairdo and cat-eye glasses. "All set, dear?"

From behind a pillow I tried to flatten myself down into the floor.

"Where have you been?" the man with the rough voice asked.

"Tee-hee," Rachel said. "I was trying on outfits, silly."

"Well, then why are you still wearing the same clothes?"

"Ummm, uh, nothing fit."

I positioned myself behind the pillows in a place where I was able to see. Another man entered the room. He stopped short. "Wow," he said, taking in Rachel, "you weren't kidding about her."

Along with Beehive, there were four men here now. None of them was Buddy Ray. So where was he? I thought about Ashley, about that monogrammed sweater and the pearls and how she was trying so hard to escape from this life. I thought about the way she looked at me, with such hope, and how, right now, she could be behind that door, in the dungeon.

Alone with Buddy Ray.

"Okay, this is perfect anyway," Beehive said. "We can do the auditions right here, right now."

"Now?" Rachel said.

"Sure, why not?"

With Beehive taking Rachel's hand, the four men all dropped onto the throw pillows. The one with a rough voice landed right near where I was hiding. His back was less than two feet from my head. I held my breath, afraid to move.

The guy near me growled, "Candy, what are you doing here?"

"Who, me?" Candy said. "Nothing."

"Then get out, will ya? And close the door behind you."

"Yes, Max. Right away."

Candy hurried out, and per the man's command, she closed the door behind her.

"Okay, Bambi," Beehive said. "Let's get you up on that stage so you can show us what you got."

"Now?"

"Right now."

Rachel slowly got up onstage. She just stood there.

"Uh, Bambi?"

"I, uh, I usually like some music," she said.

"We can sing if you want," Max said, and there was an edge in his voice now. "But I'm getting awfully impatient here."

I thought about going for my phone, but even that movement would reveal me. I tried to slowly slink off the pillow, move farther away from Max, and then . . .

Then what? What was I going to do?

Ema said, "Can I go tinkle too?"

Max waved an I-don't-care at her. I wondered what she

was up to—leaving Rachel alone—but I figured that she saw what I saw. No hope. She'd get out of the room and call 911. I remembered Juan's warning about calling the cops, but what else could we do?

I looked at the fire door. I looked at the door to the dungeon.

"Dance!" Max shouted.

And so Rachel started dancing. There was a pole up on the stage. She ignored it. Rachel was a beautiful girl. She was stunning, with the face of an angel and a body that could not only stop traffic but make it back up a little.

But she was a terrible dancer.

She started dancing as though she were the awkward cousin at a bat mitzvah.

Beehive put her hand to her chest and groaned. For a moment the men just stared in something like horror. Then they started calling out:

"What the heck is this?"

"Dance, for crying out loud."

"Shake it!"

"Use the pole."

"Wow, that's pathetic."

"Wait, are you doing the electric slide?"

I started sliding off the pillow, an inch at a time, when Max stiffened.

"Stop a second," Max said.

It was as though he sensed me. I moved a little faster, ducking behind the pillow a few yards away. Max slowly turned

his head toward me. I was out of sight now, under two pillows. I couldn't look out. I didn't even dare breathe.

"What's the matter, Max?"

"I thought I heard something."

"What?"

Max got up. He started walking toward my throw pillow.
The other guys got up too. They were moving closer to me.

"Okay," Rachel said, "my top is coming off."

That got their attention. They turned back to her. I quickly
made another dash, behind pillows near the door to the dungeon. All eyes were on Rachel. She started doing a new dance,
like some horrible imitation of John Travolta in that old
disco movie. Beehive groaned again.

That was when the door to the room burst open. Ema ran
into the room. Candy was with her.

"Bitch!" Ema shouted at Rachel. "You stole my boyfriend!"

"No!" Candy screamed. "He was mine!"

And then Rachel, catching on faster than I would have,
called back, "You want a piece of me? Come on!"

Ema ran over to Rachel and jumped up onstage. She tackled her. Candy followed, jumping onto the two of them too.
They all started screaming and shouting and fighting. For a
moment, Max and the others didn't know what to do. Other
girls ran into the room, joining the fray. The fighters rolled
onto the floor, right to the fire door, where I had no doubt
Rachel and Ema would make their escape.

Ema, you genius!

No one was paying any attention to the pillows anymore. I made my move, staying low and hurrying toward the door to the dungeon. I tried the knob. It turned. I quickly pushed the door open and disappeared into the dark behind it.

chapter 25

WHEN MY EYES ADJUSTED to the dark, I saw a staircase leading down.

The dungeon, it seemed, was in the basement.

I shut the door behind me and started down the steps. When I reached the bottom, I stopped cold. Cigarette butts littered the floor—I thought about poor Candy's arm and shivered—but that wasn't what made me pull up in shock.

There, in the middle of a cinder-block room, tied to a chair, was Ashley.

Her back was to me, her arms bound behind her. I was about to move toward her when I heard a voice say, "I thought you'd been kidnapped, Ashley."

It was Buddy Ray.

I leaned back into the dark of the stairwell, staying out of sight. I ducked low and peered out. Buddy Ray was in a corner of the room. He sat on a big tool chest closed with a padlock. He smiled at her and shook his head. He was, I couldn't help but notice, smoking a cigarette.

He also had a knife in his hand.

"Now, I know you ran away from me," Buddy Ray said, putting on a fake hurt voice. "How do you think that made me feel?"

"Let me go," Ashley said.

"You ran away. So now you'll have to be taught a lesson," Buddy Ray said with that creepy voice of his. He stood up and stepped closer to her. "I need to make sure—very sure—that you never run away from me again."

I stayed hunched in the dark, wondering what to do here. I was too far away to jump him. He had that knife and could probably call for help.

"It won't do any good," Ashley said in a voice that was oddly calm.

Buddy Ray tilted his head. "No?"

"No. Because no matter how much you hurt me, no matter what you do to me, I'll run again."

"And I'll find you again."

"And I'll run again. I don't care if you cut off my legs with that knife. I will keep trying to escape. I don't belong here."

Buddy Ray laughed, shaking his head. "You're wrong, my dear. So very wrong. What, do you think you belong in that happy little high school, wearing your little sweater, holding hands with your handsome new boyfriend? How do you think that new boyfriend would react if he knew the real you?"

That last remark hit home. I saw her stiffen. I wanted to shout out that it wouldn't matter, that I couldn't care less what her life had been before.

Buddy Ray spread his arms. "This is where you belong."

Ashley raised her head and met his eye. "No."

"You don't get it, do you?" Buddy Ray pointed at the tool chest behind him. "Do you know what's in that chest over there?"

"It doesn't matter," she said, trying so hard to sound brave.

"Oh, it matters." Buddy Ray showed her the blade in his hand. "You talk tough now." He leaned in close so that his mouth was right by her ear. I tensed up, preparing to run and try . . . I don't know . . . anything, if he touched her. Instead he dropped his voice to a whisper. "But I promise you, Ashley—I swear on all that is holy—that when I unlock that chest, when I'm done with you, you'll beg me to let you stay here and work for me."

He started walking back toward the tool chest.

My mouth was too dry to swallow. It was now or never. His back was turned. I was about to sprint out, about to make a move, when the door behind me, the one I had just gone through, began to open. I leaped back up the stairs behind it, finding the only hiding spot in the room.

Someone entered. "Boss?"

I couldn't see anything. The door was almost pressed

against me. If whoever had opened the door pushed back a little more, he would hit me square in the face.

"What?" Buddy Ray snapped. "I'm busy."

"We kinda got a situation."

I could hear the ruckus behind him.

"Can't Derrick handle it?"

"No one knows where he is."

I heard Buddy Ray sigh. "I won't be long, princess," he said.

No reply from Ashley.

Now I could hear him sprinting up the stairs. I closed my eyes, hoping against hope that he wouldn't see me. He didn't. He ran through the door, slamming it shut behind him.

I was alone with Ashley, but I was not about to sit there and consider the options. It was pretty simple: free Ashley, get out of here. I had no idea how long Buddy Ray would be gone. It could be just a few seconds.

I ran down to the dungeon. Ashley turned her head and gasped when she saw me. "Mickey?"

"We have to get you out of here."

"How did you find me?"

"No time for that now."

Ashley started weeping. I rushed over to her chair, got down on one knee, and was ready to untie her. In the movies, this always seems to take mere seconds, doesn't it? Like someone had tied up the person the same way you might tie a shoelace. But in real life, that wasn't the case. It wasn't the case at all.

Buddy Ray hadn't tied her with rope. He had used plastic cuffs, wrapping them tightly around her wrists.

I had no idea what to do. I looked around the room for something to cut them with, but there was nothing.

"Mickey?"

"Hang on, I'm just trying to figure out how to free you."

"You can't," she said, her voice defeated.

I didn't listen to her. "Wriggle your hands," I said. I tried to work the plastic with my fingers, pushing it down while she wriggled. There was absolutely no give.

"There's no time," she said. "You have to save yourself."

"No," I said.

"Mickey, he'll be back any minute. Please go. He'll just hurt me a little. He won't want to damage the goods."

I kept working at the plastic cuff. Useless. I ran over to his dreaded tool chest. I kicked the padlock, but it wouldn't give. I looked for a crowbar—anything!—but the stark room was totally bare.

Damn!

I tried one more kick. There was no way the padlock was budging. I took out my cell phone. Enough. It was time to take the risk and dial 911.

"No!" Ashley shouted. "If he sees a cop car, he'll just start killing people."

It didn't matter. I had no phone service in this cinder-block dungeon.

So now what?

Tick, tick, tick. How much longer would he be gone?

"Please, Mickey? Just listen to me, okay? There's no time. You have to go. If he hurts you, if something happens to you, I'll never be able to live with myself."

I ran back over to her and took her face in my hands. Ashley looked at me with those beautiful, imploring eyes. "I won't leave you," I said to her. "Do you hear me? No matter. I won't leave you with that monster."

Tick, tick, tick.

Wait. The plastic cuff was too strong to break. The padlock was too strong to break.

But what about a wooden chair?

"Brace yourself," I said.

"What?"

I kicked the leg of the chair. Nothing. I kicked it again. The leg started giving way. I kicked it again. The leg cracked. She was still trapped, but now maybe there was some wiggle room. If only we could move fast enough . . .

That was when I saw the door start to open.

Game over.

I knew what would happen now. Buddy Ray would see me. He would be armed with the knife. He would call behind him. Max and the other bouncers would join him as reinforcements.

We had no chance.

If you stopped and calculated the odds, there was no way to survive this.

So I didn't stop or calculate. Instead I put my head down and charged the door.

I saw no other choice. I ran with as much speed as I could. I had never played American football, but Dad and I watched whenever we could figure out how to get a game on satellite. Dad loved the Jets, which, he said, taught him the meaning of disappointment. So right now, I channeled my inner linebacker blitzing the quarterback. I didn't know if I would make it in time. I doubted I would. But I gave it everything I had.

Buddy Ray entered the room. He turned, saw me, and said, "What the . . . ?"

But that was all he said.

I crashed into him at full speed. I locked my arms around him, digging my head into his chest. We fell backward into the blue room. I raised my head a little, so now the top of my skull was under his chin. When we landed, my head pounded up into him. I could actually feel his teeth rattle and give way.

My head was still reeling from Derrick's earlier attacks. Now the pain from my own blow was so great, I worried that I might pass out. But it had been worth it. Blood was leaking out of Buddy Ray's mouth. The adrenaline helped push me through it. I made a fist and smashed into his mouth. The teeth that were already loosened gave way.

I pulled back for another punch, but I never got the chance to land it. Max, the bouncer who had been so close to me before, tackled me. He threw a knee into my rib cage. Flashes of light filled my head. It felt as though someone had just stabbed me in the lung. He reared back for another knee, the finisher, but suddenly I saw someone whack my attacker with what I later learned was the leg of a chair.

Ashley!

Max dropped off me as though he were a tree that had been chopped down. You almost wanted to shout, "Timber!" but there was no time. I rolled to my side and tried to get up, but my head was having none of it. I stood too quickly, the pain driving me back to my knees. Ashley tried to help me. I stumbled back.

"Lean on me!" Ashley shouted.

I didn't want to. I wanted her to get out, just get through that fire door, but I knew that she wouldn't listen. So I leaned on her. We took one step toward the door and then I felt a pain in my lower leg unlike anything I had ever felt before.

Buddy Ray was biting me!

I screamed and pulled away, leaving some of my skin behind. Another bouncer rounded the corner. Then another. A third came in. Max got to his feet.

The men quickly surrounded us in a circle. Ashley moved closer to me. I put a protective arm around her. Like that would do any good.

Buddy Ray staggered to his feet. He smiled at me through the blood and cracked teeth. "You," he said to me, "are going to wish you were dead."

I cringed as though I had given up. But I hadn't. With my head down, I whispered in Ashley's ear, "Follow me."

Adrenaline is a funny thing. I've read where mothers can lift cars off their children because of it. I don't know if that's true. But I know that it kept the pain away. I know that maybe it gave me a little extra strength, maybe another inch on my vertical leap. Whatever.

I ran at Buddy Ray.

He thought that I was going to attack him again, try to tackle him to the ground, so he moved to the side.

That was what I wanted.

I ran right by him. Ashley was right on my back. Yes, this wouldn't last long. The other men were already closing in. But I didn't need much time. Just two more steps.

Just to the fire door.

I banged it open with my back, grabbing Ashley with my free arm and flinging her through it. I fell back too, trying to push the door closed, but by now the other men were there. They were trying to get out. I pushed, but I couldn't hold it. No way.

And then Ema joined me. And Rachel. And Candy.

Other girls too. They pushed on the door, ten of them, maybe fifteen. They pushed on that door and held it firm and there was no way that anyone else was going to follow us out.

"Run!" Candy shouted at us. "We got this!"

"We all run," I said. "You too."

But Candy just looked at me and shook her head. "It doesn't work that way, Mickey."

"What?"

"You can't save us all."

There was a strange truth in that. I wondered about Juan, about how he chose to save Ashley and not Candy, but there was no time for that. We had to move.

In the distance I heard police cars. The commotion must have gotten their attention. They'd be here any second. A few girls scattered. I met Rachel's eye. She was with Ashley. I looked for Ema, but I didn't see her.

"We all run," I shouted again to the girls. "All of us at the same time."

And then a voice—a voice with that horrible little lisp, a voice that chilled me like no other—said, "Oh, I don't think so."

Everything stopped then. Nobody moved. It was as if the very buildings—this very alley—were suddenly holding their breath. I broke through the paralysis. I let go of the door and swiveled my head to the left.

Buddy Ray had a knife on Ema.

My heart leaped to my throat. The sirens were getting closer.

"Let her go," I said.

Buddy Ray just smiled at me. If the cracked teeth or blood was bothering him, he didn't show it. The smile had nothing behind it. No mirth, no joy, no soul. It was the scariest smile I had ever seen.

"The cops are on their way," I said. "They'll go easier on you if you let her go."

Buddy Ray laughed. "Who said I wanted it easier?"

I didn't know what to say. I was too far away to make a move. He put the knife on Ema's neck. Ema closed her eyes. Tears ran down her cheek. "Please . . . ," she said.

"You took something that belonged to me," Buddy Ray said, looking directly at me. "Now I'm going to take something that belongs to you."

"Don't," I said, my voice sounding so weak, so defeated. "If you want to get back at someone, get back at me." I raised my hands and walked toward him. "Take me instead."

I risked another step. I was still at least ten yards away. We locked eyes, Buddy Ray and me, and when I saw them, when I really took a good hard look into his eyes, my heart crumbled to dust.

Ema was doomed.

There was no reasoning here. There was no action I could take. It didn't matter that the cops were bearing down on him. For a moment, there was only him and me—and I had no doubt what he'd do next.

He was going to kill Ema.

He was going to kill her just to see my face when he did it. I couldn't talk him out of it. I couldn't reach him in time.

I was here, on the edge of victory, and so he would take Ema away from me.

It was like Buddy Ray knew it all already. I had lost my father. I was losing my mother. And now, when I finally found a real friend, I would lose her too.

He moved the knife closer to her throat. Ema squirmed, but he held her firm.

"Say good-bye," Buddy Ray said.

And then, when all hope seemed lost, with my eyes locked on Buddy Ray's—*boom*, a small truck plowed into Buddy Ray.

My mouth dropped open.

One moment Buddy Ray was standing there with a knife in his hand. The next, he was flying across the alley on the hood of a small truck.

A familiar truck.

One I'd seen once before.

A small truck with a crossed mop-head logo on the side.

As the sirens surrounded us, as the cop cars came braking to a halt, the driver's door opened, and Spoon emerged.

He pushed up his glasses, looked at the still man on the hood of the truck, and said, "Man, I really gotta learn how to drive."

Ema had called Spoon when she couldn't reach me.

"I figured maybe he could at least pick us up," she said.

I hugged her for a very long time. Rachel came over and joined us. Spoon came over too.

Police cars kept pouring in. I saw Tyrell's father arrive. My uncle Myron was there too. The Ford Taurus, I remembered now, had a GPS unit in it. Myron was able to get the coordinates. He just got them a little too late.

An ambulance came for Buddy Ray. He would live, but the girls were all talking to the police now. There would be charges. He wouldn't be free for a very long time.

With Rachel on my right and Ema on my left, I looked down the block and spotted Ashley in the distance. She was getting into Juan's van. Juan held the door open for her. Ashley looked back at me one last time and smiled. I smiled back, but there was no joy in it. Juan nodded at me. Ashley vanished into the back of the van, and as she did, I think that we both realized that we would never see each other again.

At least, that was how it felt.

I looked at Rachel. She nodded at me. Ema gave me a brave smile. Spoon wasn't sure what to do. We shared looks. My friends, I thought. The only real friends I've ever had. And yet, somehow, I knew that they were much more, that this would not be the last time we would stand together like this.

I felt overwhelmed. We all moved closer together in an almost protective cluster, looking out now as one.

"Guess what," Spoon said to me.

I swallowed hard. "What, Spoon?"

"George Washington was sterile."

chapter 26

HOURS LATER, after my leg got treated for the bite, after the police were satisfied, Uncle Myron drove me home. I expected a full-fledged grilling or a lecture, but he went easy on me. He seemed somewhat lost in his thoughts.

"You took something of a beating," he said.

I nodded.

He gripped the wheel tighter. "Is this the first time you've been hurt like this?"

I wasn't sure how to respond, so I went with the truth. "Yes."

"It will be worse in the morning. A lot worse. I have some painkillers that might help."

"Thanks."

Myron made a turn, keeping his eyes on the road. "Basketball tryouts are coming up soon."

"I know."

We fell into an uncomfortable silence. I was the one who broke it this time. "The other night, I saw you video-chatting with a woman on the computer."

Myron cleared his throat. "Oh."

"Who is she?"

"My fiancée."

That surprised me.

"She lives far away," he said. "Overseas."

"You were supposed to go to her."

Myron said nothing.

"You stayed behind," I said, "because of me."

"Don't worry about it. It will all work out."

More silence.

"Can I ask you something else?" I said.

"Okay."

"What's the deal with you and Chief Taylor?"

Myron grinned. "Chief Taylor," he said, "is a power tool."

"His son is captain of the basketball team."

"So was he," Myron said. "Years ago. He was the senior captain when I was a sophomore."

Talk about history repeating itself. "So what happened between you two?"

Myron seemed to mull it over before he shook his head.

"I'll tell you about it another time. Right now I think it's time we took care of some of your wounds."

Myron was right.

When I woke up the next day, my entire body screamed in agony. It took me ten minutes to sit up and get off the bed. My temples pulsed. My head throbbed. My ribs were so tender that breathing became a new adventure in spiked pain.

There were two pills on the nightstand next to my bed. I swallowed them down. That helped. Myron had taken the extra Ford Taurus into the shop to get the window Derrick smashed fixed. That meant I'd have to walk. The police, I figured, were still looking for Derrick. I didn't want to tell them not to waste their time.

A few hours later, I finished my walk to the Coddington Rehabilitation Institute. Christine Shippee greeted me with her arms folded across her chest.

"I told you," she said. "You can't see your mother yet."

I thought about everything. I thought about the Abeona Shelter and the work my parents clearly did for them. I thought about my dad's letter to Juan, how he wanted to give me a chance at normalcy. I thought about moving back to the United States, that drive down to San Diego, the crash of the car. I thought about that ambulance driver, the one with the sandy hair and green eyes. I thought about the way the expression on his face told me that my life was over, how

I knew right then and there that even he, this stranger with sandy hair and green eyes, knew my future better than I did.

I thought about my mom's face when she first heard that my dad was dead, how she had died on that day too. I thought about how I tried to help her—enabled, I guess—how I kept her on life support, how she clung to me, how she lied and even manipulated her only son. I thought about the spaghetti and meatballs dinner we never had. I thought about the garlic bread.

"Mickey?" Christine said. "Are you all right?"

"Just tell her I love her," I said. "Tell her I'm here and I will always be here and I will visit her every day and I will never abandon her. Tell her that."

"Okay," Christine said softly. "I will."

And then I turned and walked away.

When I reached the bottom of the drive, the black car with the license plate A30432 was waiting for me. I wasn't even surprised. The bald man got out of the passenger seat. As always he wore the dark suit and sunglasses.

He opened the back door.

Without saying a word, I got in.

chapter 27

I NEVER SAW THE DRIVER. There was a glass partition separating the front from the back. Five minutes after they picked me up, we were bouncing through the woods. I looked out. Up ahead I saw Bat Lady's garage. Just as I had witnessed that day with Ema, the bald guy got out and opened the garage door. We pulled in. The bald guy opened the door for me and said, "Follow me."

The interior of the garage looked, well, like the interior of a garage. Nothing special. The bald guy bent down and pulled open a trapdoor in the floor. He started climbing down a ladder. I trailed him. We moved through a tunnel in the direction, I assumed, of Bat Lady's house.

This, I thought, explained the light in the basement I had seen when I was in her house.

When we passed a door, I asked, "What's in there?"

He shook his head and kept going. When we reached another door, he stopped and said, "This is as far as I go."

"What's that supposed to mean?"

"It means that you see her alone."

Her.

He started back down toward the garage, leaving me alone. My head was starting to throb again. The pain meds must have been wearing off. I opened the door and found myself back inside Bat Lady's living room.

Nothing much had changed. Brown was still the room's dominant hue. The windows were still blocked by a combination of soot and planks. The grandfather clock still didn't work. The old picture of the hippies—the first place I had seen the strange butterfly design. The turntable was working now. HorsePower was playing a sad song called "Time Stands Still." And there, in the middle of the room, dressed in the same white gown I had seen her in just a few short days ago, was the Bat Lady.

She smiled at me. "You did well, Mickey."

I wasn't in the mood for more cat and mouse games. "Gee, thanks. Really. I mean, I have no idea what I did or what's going on here, but thanks."

"Sit with me."

"No, I'm good here."

"You're angry. I understand."

"You said my father was alive."

Bat Lady sat on a couch that looked as though it had been ready for the scrap heap during the Eisenhower administration. Her hair was still ridiculously long, cascading down her back and almost touching the seat cushion. She picked up a large book, an old photo album, and held it on her lap.

"Well?" I said.

"Sit, Mickey."

"Is my father still alive?"

"It's not a simple question."

"Sure it is. He's either dead or he's alive. Which is it?"

"He is alive," she said, with a smile that seemed somewhere south of sane, "in you."

I never wanted to smack an old woman before, but boy, I did now. "In me?"

"Yes."

"Oh, please. What is this, *The Lion King*? That's what you meant when you said he was alive?"

"I meant exactly what I said."

"You told me that my father was alive. Now you're giving me some New Age mumbo jumbo about him living in me."

I turned away, blinked back the tears. I felt crushed. I felt stupid. Some crazy old lady rants stuff I know not to be true—and yet I choose to hold on to her words like a drowning man to a life preserver. Man, was I an idiot or what?

"So he's dead," I said.

"People die, Mickey."

"Good answer," I said with as much sarcasm as I could muster.

"Nothing about what we do is simple," she said. "You want a yes or no. But there is no yes or no. No black or white. It is all gray."

"There is life or death," I said.

She smiled. "What makes you sure of that?"

I had no idea how to respond.

"We save who we can," she said. "We can't save everyone. Evil exists. You can't have an up without a down, a right without a left—or a good without an evil. Do you understand?"

"Not really, no."

"Your father came to this house when he was about your age. It changed him. He understood his calling."

"To work for you?"

"To work with us," she said, correcting me.

"And become, what, part of the Abeona Shelter?"

She did not reply.

"So you were the ones who rescued Ashley."

"No," she said. "You did that."

I sighed. "Can you stop talking in circles?"

"There is a balance. There are choices. We rescue a few, not all, because that is what we can do. Evil remains. Always. You can combat it, but you can never fully defeat it. You settle for small victories. If you overreach, you lose everything. But every life matters. There is an old saying:

'He who saves one life saves the world.' So we pick and choose."

"You pick and choose who gets rescued and who doesn't?"

"Yes," Bat Lady said. "Take Candy, for example."

That surprised me. "You know about Candy?"

She didn't bother replying. "If we had chosen to help her, the odds are that Candy would have ended up no better off. She has no skills, not much intelligence, and would never be able to be mainstreamed into school or society. She would probably have ended up back with Buddy Ray or someone similar."

"You can't know that," I said.

"Of course you can't know. But you play the odds. You save who you can and you mourn those you can't. When you follow this calling, your heart gets ripped apart every day. You make the world better in increments, not grand designs. You make choices. Do you understand?"

"Choices," I said.

"Yes."

"Like my father made a choice to leave the Abeona Shelter. Like my father didn't want this life for me."

"Exactly, he made a choice." Bat Lady looked up at me and tilted her head. "How did that work out for him?"

I said nothing.

"With choices come consequences," she said.

I didn't know what to say to that. I looked out the back,

through the kitchen, toward the garden. "You have a tombstone in your backyard."

She said nothing.

"The initials E.S.," I said. "Is Elizabeth Sobek buried there?"

"Lizzy," Bat Lady said.

"What?"

"Her name was Lizzy. She preferred Lizzy."

"Is she buried in your yard?"

"Sit down, Mickey."

"I'm fine standing right here. Is Lizzy Sobek, the girl who rescued all those kids in the Holocaust, buried in your yard, yes or no?"

Now there was steel in her voice. "Sit down, Mickey."

Bat Lady looked up at me, and I did as she asked. Dust came off the couch. She put her left arm out and pulled up her sleeve. The tattoo was faded but you could still read it:

A30432

For a moment, I couldn't speak. Then I managed to say, "You?"

She nodded. "I'm Lizzy Sobek."

I sat there in silence as she opened the photograph album. "You want to know how this all began. I will tell you. And then maybe you will understand about your father."

She pointed to the first picture in the photo album. It was an old black-and-white shot of four people. "This was my family. My father's name was Samuel. My mother's name was Esther. That's my older brother, Emmanuel, with the bow tie. Such a handsome boy. So smart, so kind. He was eleven when this picture was taken. I was eight. I look happy, don't you think?"

She did. She had been a beautiful child.

"You know what happened next," she said.

"World War Two."

"Yes. For a while we survived in the Lodz ghetto. That was in Poland. My father was a wonderful man. Everyone loved him. They were drawn to him. Your father, Mickey, was a lot like him. But that's not important right now. For a long time we managed to escape and stay hidden. I won't go into the details, the horrors that even now, even all these years later, I, who witnessed it, cannot believe. Suffice to say that eventually someone sold us out. My family was captured by the Nazis. We were put on a train for Auschwitz."

Auschwitz. Just the word made me shiver. I actually reached out for her hand, but Bat Lady stiffened.

"Please let me get through this," she said. "Even after all these years, it is hard."

"I'm sorry," I said.

She nodded, looked off again. "When my family arrived at Auschwitz, they separated us. I found out later that my mother and my brother, Emmanuel, were taken immediately to the gas chambers. They were dead within hours. My father was brought to a work camp. I was spared. I still don't know why."

She turned the page of her photo album. There were more pictures of her family, of Esther and Emmanuel living lives that were snuffed out for reasons that still no one could fathom. She didn't look at the pictures. She just stared straight ahead.

"Again I won't go into the details of what it was like in the concentration camp," she said. "I will skip ahead six weeks to the day my father and some other workers overpowered the guards. A group of eighteen men broke free. The news spread around camp like wildfire. I was thrilled, of course, but now I felt more alone than ever. I was so scared. That night, I sat up and cried even though I thought that I had no more tears left. I felt ashamed. And there, as I lay alone crying, my father came and found me. He came to my bunk and whispered, 'I would never leave you behind, my little dove.'"

Bat Lady smiled at the memory.

"We escaped together. My father and me. We joined the other men in the woods. I can't tell you how that felt, Mickey. How it felt to be free. It was like being held underwater for a long time and finally being able to draw that first breath when you hit the surface. Being with my father, trying to figure a way to join the resistance, it was the last great moment I remember. And then . . ."

The smile faded away now. I waited, not wanting her to stop, not wanting to hear the rest of her story. It was almost as if someone had turned the lights down. A chill filled the room.

"Then he found us."

She turned and looked at me.

"Who?" I said.

"The Butcher of Lodz," she said in a harsh whisper. "He was Waffen-SS."

I held my breath.

"He found us in the woods. Surrounded us. He made us dig a pit and fill it with lime. Then he lined us all up next to it. Our backs were to his men. The Butcher looked at my father, then at me. He laughed. My father begged for my life to be spared. The Butcher looked at me a long time. I will never forget the expression on his face. Finally he shook his head. I remember my father turned back around and took my hand. He said to me, 'Don't be frightened, my little dove.' Then the Butcher and his men shot us, firing right straight down the line, but at the last second, my father pushed me into the pit and moved just a little to his right, to block me from the bullets. His dead body landed on top of me. I stayed there all night, in the cold, with my father on top of me. I don't know how much time passed. Night turned to day. Eventually I crawled out and escaped into the woods."

She stopped. I waited, feeling my body shake from her

tale. When she didn't speak again, I said, "So you found safety. That's when you started rescuing children."

She suddenly looked exhausted. "One day, I will explain more."

Silence.

"I don't get it," I said.

She turned and faced me.

"You said this story would tell me about my father. I don't see how it did."

"I'm trying to make you understand."

"Understand what?"

"My father. He made a choice. His life for mine. I had to make good on that. I had to make his choice into the right one."

I felt the tears well in my eyes. "But your father was murdered. Mine died in an accident."

She lowered her eyes, and for a moment, I thought that maybe I could see the little girl under all those years. "When the war ended—when the world believed that I was dead—I searched for the Butcher of Lodz. I wanted to bring him to justice for what he did. I contacted groups that search for ex-Nazis."

I didn't know where she was going with this, but I could feel the hairs on the back of my neck stand up. "Did you find him?"

She looked off again, not responding to my question. "You see, sometimes I still see his face. I see him on the streets, or out my window. He haunts my sleep, even now, even all these years later. I still hear his laugh before he killed my father. Still. But mostly . . ." She stopped.

"Mostly what?" I said.

She turned and met my eye. "Mostly I remember the way he looked at me when my father asked him to spare me. Like he knew."

"Knew what?"

"That my life, the life of a girl named Lizzy Sobek, was over now. That I would survive but never be the same. So I kept searching for him. Through the years and even decades. I finally found his real name and an old photograph of him. All the Nazi hunters told me to relax, not to worry, that the Butcher was dead, that he had been killed in action in the winter of 1945."

And then it happened. She turned the page and pointed at the photograph of the Butcher in his Waffen-SS uniform. I saw right away that he hadn't died, that the Nazi hunters had been wrong. You see, I had seen this man before.

He had sandy hair and green eyes, and last time I saw him, he was taking my father away in an ambulance.

ACKNOWLEDGMENTS

I had a blast writing *Shelter*, and I can't tell you what a thrill it is to have you as a reader.

I want to thank my great Penguin YA team: Shanta Newlin, Emily Romero, Elyse Marshall, Erin Dempsey, Lisa DeGroff, Courtney Wood, Greg Stadnyk, Ryan Thomann, Jen Loja and Shauna Fay—not to mention the usual suspects, Brian Tart, Ben Sevier and Christine Ball.

I also need to thank Maria Cannon's students at George Washington Middle School for helping with the cover.

My kids and their friends were all tremendous inspirations. Yes, I eavesdropped, so you might see yourself on some of these pages. Sorry!

I especially want to thank my wonderful editor Jen Besser and my dear friend and new publisher, Don Weisberg. And of course, my wife, Anne, who knew that it was finally time to write this book.

I'm hoping to write more books about Mickey Bolitar and the gang. To stay in touch with us, please visit MickeyBolitar.com.